Also by Ellis Sharp

Novels

The Dump
Unbelievable Things
Walthamstow Central
Intolerable Tongues
To Wetumpka
Lamees Najim
The Orwell Girl
Neglected Writer
What Vronsky Did Next
Alice in Venice
Full English
The Riddle
Month of the Drowned Dog
Pig Tale
Concrete Impressions

Short Fiction

The Aleppo Button
Lenin's Trousers
(with Mac Daly) *Engels on Video*
To Wanstonia
Driving My Baby Back Home
Aria Fritta
Quin Again and other stories
Dead Iraqis: Selected Short Stories

Non-Fiction

Sharply Critical
Twenty-Twenty

ELLIS SHARP

NIGHT ARCHITECTURE

Zoilus Press

A Zoilus Press paperback
First published in Great Britain by Zoilus Press in 2024

© Ellis Sharp 2024

A CIP catalogue record for this book is available from the British Library.

ISBN 9781838489830

Cover design by The Ever-Shifting Subject

Typeset by Electrograd

ZOILUS PRESS
York, England

NIGHT ARCHITECTURE

Contents

NIGHT ARCHITECTURE

Part One

It was an ultra hot day in May and thirteen tornadoes had struck Italy.

As his plane taxied away from the terminal building at Schiphol, Aaron Gould couldn't pretend he cared. Rome was flooded, it would do the city good. He'd never liked its hot dusty cluttered streets. That tiresome omnipresent heritage of cracked and leaning stone. The place needed cleansing and tidying up. In a word: *modernising*.

As for Venice. It held certain strong and pleasant memories but he'd no particular wish to go back. This morning's much-recorded sight of the Rialto being wrenched apart, then collapsing into the Grand Canal, did not move him. It was a cliché – an imitation of a scene from a disaster movie he'd seen before. Besides, the bridge would get rebuilt. He smiled faintly at a fresh thought. There might be a business opportunity there...

Aaron stared out of the window. It was a fact that soon the headlines would move on to something else. Nobody really cared much about Italy except the Italians. A shrill, easily-excited people. Also, climate catastrophe porn was a worn-out thrill. Everyone was sated. To be interesting it needed something bigger than the fall of an old bridge or a tumbling Roman temple. It would be amusing to see the Eiffel Tower do cartwheels and huge fragments of Meccano showering central Paris. Plus it was high time the Louvre's vulgar glass pyramid was levelled.

In bright sunlight the jet approached the underpass. That acute external glare exposed the myriad tiny scratches on his window. It made the shadow of the moving wing below him precise and clean.

Above, the windows of vehicles passing along the road briefly flashed. And then, as the aircraft entered the underpass, the brightness stopped. The world beyond his window darkened.

Moments later the crawling plane emerged from this gloomy passageway. Surprised, Aaron saw that the blue sky was now almost gone. A sheet of dark boiling cloud was racing overhead, shutting out the sunshine. His cabin window was suddenly hit by a fistful of snowflakes. Most bounced off, but from behind them came more. Now flakes began to build along one side of the outer casing.

The plane rolled on at the speed of a golf cart. It shook the snow off. The terminal building receded, then dropped from sight behind a row of parked jets. That was the downside to Amsterdam. Schiphol was an enormous airport and it was always like this. Invariably it seemed to take twenty minutes or more of monotonous manoeuvring to get to that point where you either finally arrived or at last departed. City Airport was so very much quicker.

Almost there.

It was now uniformly grey out there, though the wall of snow had gone.

The pilot instructed the cabin crew to take their seats.

Aaron felt generally good. They were at least now really on their way. Mercifully, there had been no last-minute event to delay the plane. Plus he was lucky. His scheduled flight wasn't until the evening but the airline had phoned. They'd offered him an earlier unlisted one. A ghost flight, needed to fulfil an airport contract. He'd read about them but never been on one.

The plane was almost empty. Just five other passengers. He'd never travelled on a passenger jet this size with so few people.

Another faint smile: a sudden memory of that old black and white movie he'd watched with Sarah in his room all those years ago. He could still recall the title and how it started, but not the ending. Did everyone survive or were they all killed? That bit he'd forgotten. *The Night My Number Came Up*. A good title but not an outstanding movie. It was plot-driven, with forgettable characters. Not one of those films you needed to see again.

Near the front a pair of young trouser-suited businesswomen, chattering away like finches. Three rows back a weird guy wearing a hood and dressed in a dark gown. It made him look like a monk.

Maybe he *was* a monk. There was an enclosed Benedictine order of nuns in the countryside north-west of Diss, so maybe there was a monastery tucked away there too.

Lost Horizon. That was another ancient monochrome movie which started off with a handful of Westerners on a plane where things started to go wrong... Variations on a theme. Aaron was unperturbed. *Airplane!* was the one he remembered best. The singing nun banging her guitar on the heads of the seated passengers. The smile of satisfaction on the face of the inflatable pilot. (He smiled at the thought that he'd smiled that smile himself on many occasions.)

Four rows back a businessman in a blue suit, fortyish, stared down into his phone. After that a very old woman, wrapped in the drab grey and mud-coloured clothing favoured by the geriatric class. Her stark white hair cropped short. She already had her eyes closed when he boarded and made his way past her to his seat. Her face had seemed draped in layers of wrinkled, liver-spotted skin. Repulsive.

Aaron sincerely hoped she wasn't going to die in her seat. He had once been on a flight to Berlin and twenty minutes after take-off a passenger had suffered cardiac arrest. The subsequent inconvenience had been extremely tiresome.

He liked his chosen seat. The last third of the jet's interior belonged to him alone.

Aaron had a very slight phobia about people who sat behind him on planes which weren't full. Maybe it was a 9/11 thing. Irrational but inescapable. He wouldn't have liked the hooded guy to be behind him.

And now the jet was turning on to the final runway.

The engine noise deepened and grew louder, louder, louder. The plane jerked forward, the line of lights beside the runway shot past, his ears flinched at the change in pressure.

They were airborne.

It was at this moment that Aaron glimpsed the twister.

As Schiphol dropped away he saw the huge dark swaying column moving in the space between two low warehouses near the airport's perimeter. It drifted across a small car park. Vehicles flew silently upward and crashed against the adjacent building.

And then the plane banked, heading for the coast, and he could no longer see it. Gaining height the jet rushed through layers of wispy cloud. Then the cloud melted away and Aaron observed below a patchwork of fields and a length of dark meandering river.

Seatbelts off.

The stewardess began to make her way down the aisle, distributing her treats. Soon she stood above him, thirty maybe, very pale smooth skin, piercing blue eyes. Beautiful, especially with those slightly prominent finely sculpted cheekbones.

'Did you see the tornado?' Aaron said.

'In Italy, yes. So sad.'

'No, I meant at Schiphol. Just now.'

She looked puzzled. 'Sir, there are no tornadoes at Schiphol. Would you like a biscuit?' She held out a cellophane-wrapped digestive.

Aaron declined it but accepted the pouch of ice-cold water. He swallowed it down while admiring the stewardess's departing rump.

Now the ragged Dutch coastline gave way to the grey North Sea and a field of spinning wind turbines. There were hundreds of them.

And there it was again, the twister, as though it had hurried to catch up with the plane. But that was surely not possible.

This tornado was moving faster than the other one. It slid between a lane of turbines, then veered and swallowed one. The great blades buckled and fell inwards. Seconds later the twister spat them out. Even from this height Aaron could see the white splashes as the pieces hit the surface of the sea.

He glanced up the aisle. The stewardess wasn't there. The two women were still talking intensely. The hooded figure's head had tipped forwards, as if he was asleep. The businessman was hunched over his device. The old woman was barely visible, as if she had shrunk a little since the start of the flight.

No one else seemed to have noticed the tornado. Aaron glanced back at it but it could no longer be seen. The turbine field had dropped away. Now there was just an expanse of sea, empty apart from a solitary tanker moving in the direction of the German coast.

The weather had changed, too. The clouds had gone and the sky was a uniform blue. The sunlight changed the sea's slate surface to indanthrene blue.

Aaron yawned and opened the copy of *The Times* he'd bought at the airport. He skipped the news pages and went straight to the arts. *Vantablack*, the new show at The Serpentine, looked really interesting. Plus there was a new Howard Jacobson. The reviewer, Hadley Bloodsmith, was ecstatic. *A Polished Toad* sounded wonderful. Howard – a lovely man, he'd met him a few times – really had his finger on the pulse of these dark times. Plus there was a review of Thomas Stopper's new play, *My Genocide Waltz*. It sounded unmissable. Maureen Lipshitz as Eva Braun, Helen Midden as Himmler, Edward Arsan as Goebbels, Steve Barking as the camp commander – several of the great actors of our time. And some guys from the BBC symphony orchestra were doing the live music.

Aaron decided to phone his secretary the moment he landed and get her to book tickets.

He skimmed through the business section, then laid the paper on the empty seat beside him. He yawned again and closed his eyes. He felt a sudden exhaustion. Hardly surprising really. It had been a hectic couple of days. He'd decided to break the journey back with a stopover in Amsterdam. He was on his final chapter and he needed to refresh his memory of *The Night Watch*.

It wasn't simply the image – Rembrandt's composition – that mattered. It was the painting's texture he needed to absorb. Those cobweb-thin brush strokes around the rims of hats. The ribs of paint that marked out the patterns of a knuckle.

He checked into a hotel near the Rijksmuseum and was there next morning when it opened. Briefly alone in front of the enormous canvas he felt the moment to be – humblebrag! – historic. He scrutinised the great painting close-up and took photographs. As the first tourists began to trickle into the room, he retreated to a bench, where he furiously jotted notes. Apart from their utility to his unfinished chapter they would be useful to a future biographer.

Later, he drank coffee beside a canal and in a bookshop bought a volume of old photographs of the city. Amsterdam was one of Aaron's ten favourite cities. He liked the way the water took hold of the buildings and twisted them. The bell-shaped outlines fell from on high, becoming tongues and nipples. The city's notorious aspect shone from the restless ditches which quartered these spotless bourgeois neighbourhoods.

By nightfall Aaron had disposed of most of the cash in his wallet. He used his American Express only for the hotel, the book and at a restaurant. By midnight, after a short private familiar excursion, he was showered and in bed.

Aaron opened his eyes. They were approaching the English coast. East Anglia lay under a faint haze, blurring its features. It was just possible to distinguish The Wash and the curve of the coastline as it stretched from King's Lynn to Great Yarmouth and beyond. That white speck they were passing over was the lighthouse at Southwold, and north of it the pitiful strip of grey tape was dismal Lake Lothing. Aaron had once abseiled down Southwold lighthouse for charity. Esther had been horrified and urged him not to. But it had been surprisingly easy. And of course it was brilliant PR – it educated the Suffolk population that not only was the county graced by the presence of a *prize-winning architect* who lived locally but he was also a really great guy.

The plane descended to that entity laughably known as Norwich International Airport. It was as minimalist as Biarritz or, for that matter, Inverness and Stornoway. But there was a lot to be said for minimalism. These were brisk, no-fuss airports.

They sank down over the relief road and its flow of toy vehicles. Old Catton flashed by. There was the loud thud of the wheels hitting the runway.

A minute later they were taxiing towards the glass fronted terminal building, where faces stared out from the coffee lounge.

Aaron followed the others out of the plane. The stewardess stood by the exit uttering her bright-smile thanks to everyone for choosing KLM. *Have a safe onward journey.*

As he approached her he reached out his hand, as if to shake hers. She responded automatically. But instead of gripping her hand he pressed his business card into her palm.

'Call me sometime when you're staying in the city. We should meet up for dinner.'

And then he was past her and down the steps, taking with him the memory of her look of surprise and slight perplexity.

Outside the plane the Norfolk air was treacly thick. The silver flank of the jet radiated pulses of heat.

The runway apron shimmered, twisting and distorting the outlines of the ancient planes in the air museum north-west of the perimeter fence.

As he hurried after the other passengers into the arrivals lounge Aaron discovered he couldn't get a signal. Odd. The two businesswomen were gabbling into their phones. As was blue suit. As was the hooded man, who had now put it down, exposing his bare scalp.

Hood-man looked astonishingly like Yuval Noah Harari. It couldn't be, surely. Just a pale, shaven-headed lookalike. But he even had that faintly otherworldly appearance of the original. Harari was a great guy and a phenomenal thinker but Aaron had always found him a bit creepy – you sort of felt that in a space drama he'd be the quiet, efficient crew member who turned out to be a murderous android.

For fuck's sake – even the representative of the living dead was whispering into her phone. As he overtook her Aaron noted that daylight didn't improve her appearance.

The reflected sunlight on the terminal's great panes of sheet glass was painfully bright. Aaron's contacts list dissolved in the restless glitter on his screen. It only reappeared once he'd followed the ones ahead of him and entered the low grey building. In its interior he tried to make his call. But still he couldn't get a signal.

He continued briskly along the corridor that led to border control. A sealed glass door labelled NO ENTRY supplied Aaron with a momentary image of himself. Linen jacket, white shirt, casual smart. Forty-something. A successful professional, on business.

His dark doppelganger slid by and vanished into the door frame.

People said he looked like the young Leonard Cohen. The same nose framed by the same twin grooves. The rich dark hair, the smile. Plus of course the same dry sense of humour.

No one had recognised him on the plane or at Schiphol, which was unsurprising. The profession in which his name was known was not one which commanded public attention. Architecture would never be as muscularly sexy as tennis or cookery, let alone acting or singing.

In the hall at the end of the corridor a short queue had formed by the only staffed passport booth. When he was next but one Aaron reached for his passport. It occurred to him it was the same colour as the dried blood he'd walked past on that silent street three days earlier.

'Where did you start your journey?'

A trick question. Aaron knew better than to say Amsterdam. That answer might result in a search for drugs. He naturally carried none on his person or in his baggage but the mere fact of the fingered scrutiny would be tiresome. Those charged with such tasks liked to take their time. He still recalled the occasion when waiting to board he was removed from the departures lounge so that his leather belt might be swabbed for explosives. A preposterous suspicion and he had a shrewd idea why he alone had been selected for this tiny humiliation. But it was best to say nothing; best simply to be charming and let the Neanderthals get on with their hobby. In their spare time they probably made models of the *Titanic* out of matchsticks. The Neanderthals liked nothing better than truculence and resistance. Such behaviour brought their allies running with handcuffs dangling from their waists.

'Ben Gurion.'

The man in the booth gave him a curt look and returned the passport.

Aaron went to the baggage carousel, where his scarlet Samsonite case was already circulating. Still no signal. It was only when he stepped out of the building that he finally managed to get through to his P.A. Her voice seemed remote and thin, and bursts of crackling intruded into their brief conversation. He stood there in the heat gazing at his lopsided shadow and made two other calls. When they were over he went off to the rank to take a taxi into town.

He flopped into the first cab in the line. The cracked leather seating crackled as he sank into it. The leather was coated in a thin sheet of transparent plastic. Protection from vomit, Aaron supposed. The cab interior held a faint sickly odour, in which sour lingering twists of smoked tobacco did battle with lemon-scented air freshener. Mercifully, the air conditioning was on its highest setting, emitting a faint continuous rattle below the rush of cool air.

'Drop me at Tombland, will you?'

'OK, guv.'

They left the airport and a minute later turned left at the Fifers Lane lights. The sun's dazzle made Aaron suddenly aware of a hairline scratch across the cab windscreen and a spider's web sparkling as it stretched and swayed beneath the driver's wing mirror.

'Going to Carrow Road on Saturday?' the driver wanted to know.

No he was not.

Aaron had once attended a football match. It had been a disagreeable experience. Two hours on a hard plastic chair exposed to a freezing wind. It seemed more like the prelude to an interrogation than an entertainment. That monstrous tribal rabble known as 'fans' propelled themselves into the air with a Nuremberg roar when their team succeeded, or almost succeeded, in tapping the ball into the other team's goal. As if it mattered – as if it changed *anything* – which gang of eleven educationally-impoverished booted dullards won.

Moreover the available nourishment during the intermission was a choice of sloppy abominations layered with grease, curls of blackened fried onion, and sauces resembling Technicoloured diarrhoea.

'Going somewhere nice on holiday?'

This man – Cockney via Essex, judging by his rodent accent, display of sooty chest hair, and neck chain of Trump Tower gold – had all the impudent inquisitive loquacity of a barber. Was it loneliness or a terror of that mausoleum-silent void that lies at the heart of things that made these oafs seek to fill the scented air with threads of fatuous chatter?

'No.'

Not true. But he saw no reason to share his future itineraries. The forthcoming week on Jura at David's estate, on the opposite side to where solo or paired nervy intense pilgrims trickled north on the Barnhill trail, holding their coffee-stained copies of a badly-written, wildly over-valued Cold War adventure fantasy.

The imminent fortnight in a high-end hotel apartment on the Goldeneye estate. This was largely to humour Esther, who adored solar radiation.

The September week in a clifftop chateau overlooking the ocean, just outside Biarritz. The food there would be very, very good. *Fruits de mer*. Langoustines and oysters to die for.

They passed through Old Catton, then swerved south at a ring road roundabout.

Now the driver was sharing his thoughts about the extreme weather in Italy. It was his very strongly held opinion that there had always been patches of very bad weather. No apocalyptic conclusions, he philosophised, should be distilled from this indubitable fact. 'Roadworks,' he added, adverting to his convoluted route. 'Everywhere.' Decorating his firm beliefs with many adjectives, he blamed the Council. The Council, he asserted bitterly, was one of the leading regiments in the local war against the motorist.

On they rat-runned, bumping down humped streets of terraced housing, past small grey malnourished parks, dodging the clusters of gridlock. At length they reached the roundabout by the puppet theatre. A minute later Aaron was paying the driver and setting off along Tombland to his office on the far side of the castle.

Aaron Gould Architecture...

Located on a steep ancient street rising from an old route through the city centre, the tall slender structure of glass and steel soared up between a deconsecrated Tudor church and what had once been an eighteenth-century inn. Aaron had designed it himself.

There had been protests at the time it was first mooted – complaints that it was too tall, too out of keeping with its surroundings. That, crucially, it intruded on the nearby dominant outline of the Norman keep. It was enough to make anyone of refined sensibility sigh, scowl and shake that bony helmet enclosing the soft matter of a seething, advanced brain.

Protests. The predictable wearisome provincial chorus of sentimentalists, philistines and Nimbies. The *Telegraph* wailers and *Guardian* whiners. They snivelled that his proposal degraded the neighbourhood. Even *Private Eye* got in on the act (though he knew who'd written that particular column and it was pure professional jealousy and malice).

These complaints were absurd. What exactly was being spoiled? The church, festooned with lurid advertising, was a craft centre selling kitsch of every variety. This was the place to go when in need of a model Buddha or a painted wooden seagull mass-produced in a South Korean factory. As for the inn... That remained to this day a wine bar and restaurant for the budget-minded bourgeoisie.

In due course – it was as inevitable as spring following winter – the protests and petitions faded. The planning committee (thankfully made up of men of vision, who understood that commerce should be their guide) welcomed such an innovative contribution to the city's cluttered hub of chain stores.

They – and he – had been vindicated. Today, The Gould Building was recognised as one of the earliest examples of the new aesthetic of Night Architecture. People came to take its photograph. They had to come twice, of course. Firstly to take a picture by day, showing the faintly gherkin-like shape and the curving panels of brushed steel. *Matisse-like* was the orthodox appreciation. But to return after dark was to experience the revelation. Now the structure seemed a different building altogether: slimmer, more like a rocket from a 1950s science fiction illustration, resting on supports like fins, with two sleek smaller fins at its waist.

It was an optical illusion, of course. That was what night architecture was all about: the use of materials which dimmed parts of a façade by day, leading the eyes to focus on other aspects, and by night illuminating those muted elements. Steel, glass, mirrored panelling and concealed lighting were all part of the mix. The architecture might be complex in design and implementation, yet the basic principles were simple. That was what had made his book *Night Architecture* a classic. A relatively short text – novella length, really – articulated an idea which no one in this sphere of human knowledge had ever articulated before. *Reversal.*

Smiling, Aaron stepped into the reception area and approached the desk. Rachel, the new girl, greeted him enthusiastically. 'Welcome back, Mr Gould! A good trip?'

'Very much so. Enjoyable and productive.'

Rachel gazed up at him with her deep-set blue eyes. Her jaw seemed in some way connected to her breasts, because as she tilted it the sharp curves of her upper torso seemed to tighten.

What a dark attractive girl she was, Aaron thought. Her eyes sparkled. Her display of cleavage pushed close to the limits of modesty. It seemed both to tease and to invite. Aaron made a mental note to make sure she accompanied him to a conference at some point later in the year.

Exposing her perfect white teeth again she said, 'I'll tell Becky you've arrived.' She picked up the landline. It was one of those post-modern retro see-thru phones, exposing a nest of bright wiring.

He left his case with Rachel and took the stairs to his penthouse office. It was a stiff ascent which he chose partly to maintain his dedication to physical fitness and partly because he had a fear of elevators. He'd once become trapped in a crowded one at Covent Garden tube station. It broke down and it took an eternity before its human load was released back into the world. Standing pressed close to strangers had been unpleasant, especially when someone nearby had farted. A sulphurous stench with hints of curry passing along a sewer filled his nostrils until that moment when a wooden side panel magically opened and a London Transport man ushered everyone into a dark, narrow, oil-smeared stairwell that led upward to a door off the ticket office. After that grim, unpleasant experience Aaron did his best to avoid elevators.

He reached the top. He noted a slight increase in his heart rate (but of course that might simply have been Rachel's doing).

His P.A., Becky Golding, was standing in the doorway, holding the door open for him. 'Welcome back, Aaron.'

She looked gorgeous as always, in a simple floral dress that hung down below her knees. The light was behind her and he could see the stark outline of her thighs through the pattern of interlocking tendrils and yellow petals. His heart, which had been settling down (along with another disturbed organ lower down), began to speed up again as he realised that Becky did not appear to be wearing knickers. Or was this simply his over-active imagination?

Slipping off his jacket, he moved towards his immense teak desk. Aaron confirmed to Becky that his trip abroad to collect the prize and do some business had been great, really great. He took a small box from his briefcase and handed it to her. 'For you – a souvenir.'

Becky cried out with pleasure.

She was, Gould appreciated, one of those rare, naturally ebullient women, whose eyes always seem to be on fire and who are forever charmed by small, inconsequential things. Today, among the constantly replenished supply of small, new nuggets of delight, was this bottle of perfume. Admittedly it had been very expensive.

'Oh Aaron,' she breathed. 'Thank you so, so much.' She opened the bottle and shook a few drops on to the back of her little wrist. She sniffed it. 'Divine.'

She held her wrist out, inviting the attention of his nostrils. And then she kissed him.

Afterwards, she brought him a cappuccino and told him what had arrived for his attention during his seven-day absence from the office.

He sipped it, standing. The froth was dusted with chocolate shaped into an 'A'.

From this height the studded spire of the cathedral was visible beyond the castle keep and the sloping transparent roof panels of the adjacent shopping mall.

The mall was a design disaster, Aaron felt – both from the outside and in its banal, orthodox caverns of harshly lit retail experience. But he kept that opinion private. You do not get on in life by telling people where they have gone wrong. Diplomacy and charm are the secrets of success. Aaron had never had any wish to alienate the local council or its planning department, with whom he had always had excellent relations. They in turn basked in his presence in the city. It was generally felt to be one in the eye for London that a top architect like Aaron Gould remained true to his roots. Others in his position would have long ago left for an office overlooking the Thames.

In the world of architecture and in the lifestyle features of the corporate press Aaron Gould was very well known. It had all started with his first book, written when he was only twenty-nine. It had become a classic. The very concept of 'night architecture' was stunningly innovative. To design a building for its appearance by night as well as by day was unique in itself. But that the design for night should in some sense *expose* the aesthetics of the daytime building – this was truly revolutionary. As he'd explained, night architecture was about a reconfiguration of the daytime appearance of a built structure. Or as he once put it in a throwaway remark to an interviewer, the first task of the architect is to dress a building as if it is a beautiful woman. Then, at night, one strips away the elegant fabric to show the delightful body beneath it.

It was a remark which had attracted accusations of sexism and one which he now very much regretted. Mercifully, the dissent was confined largely to a handful of screeching harpies on social media. One could comfortably afford to ignore such distant tiny cracklings. The corporate media was what counted, and there he was a shining giant.

Aaron had first expressed his concept through a series of stunning houses. His first, Jack's House (as it came to be known) was for the famously extravagant social media billionaire Jack Fattberg. This dazzling structure was embedded in a rock outcrop in the Mojave Desert. In the heat of the day Jack's House was a mass of delicate interlocking curves, as female-contoured as the rust-coloured rocks which protruded from the surrounding sandy wastes. By night the house softened into a distinctive, rippling oval, with a V-shaped penthouse suite. Illuminated swirls of water passed along troughs which opened up at night beneath the starry sky.

Lighting was only part of the trick. Even the sceptics were won over by the way Jack's House articulated an astonishing duality. With night architecture you got two houses for the price of one.

Others followed, including Aaron Gould's own new home on the Suffolk coast. Sadly, the construction of Serena Lodge had been anything but serene. The original design had attracted controversy when the local authority handed over public land for the project. Worse, it was land which had been designated a Site of Special Scientific Interest. The planning department, fortunately, took a pragmatic view. Realistically the neighbourhood was not short of woodland. The deer and that family of rare toads could be easily relocated. Sadly, the planning committee's decision to divert half a mile of public footpath was over-ruled by the Planning Inspectorate. The government declined to get involved. The constituency was solidly Conservative and swamp-dwellers have a tendency to become excitable over habitat issues. It meant tunnelling a section of the drive up to the house. Maddeningly, that added a quarter to the construction costs. No matter. The property had doubled in value since being built five years ago.

By day, from the Angel Marsh side, Serena Lodge resembled a grey and silver space ship which had gently settled itself among the pines beside the Blyth estuary. At night the craft folded itself up ('like a butterfly' as one journalist brilliantly put it) and became no more than a series of ridges, corrugating a gentle slope beside the whispering reeds. Only a savage could fail to see the beauty of it. Soon, journalists were queuing to interview Britain's most dynamic and successful young architect in his futuristic home. A dozen glossies and newspaper supplements had featured Aaron and Esther Gould at home. They made a handsome couple standing on their bedroom terrace, outlined against a background of straw-coloured marshland and the distant narrow river.

'There's a conference invitation,' Becky said. 'Brazil.' Aaron flinched. He'd been there several times before. The place bored him.

There was a request for an interview from a journalist on a French magazine. And his publishers had written, anxious to know when his new book would be completed.

Becky added: 'Ben wants a word before you head on home.'

Aaron kissed her on the cheek and let the palm of his right hand lightly brush her bottom. No, definitely no knickers.

He said he'd see her after the weekend. Then, briefcase in hand, he headed down to the floor below to see his second in command, Benjamin Lezard. He ran the show when Aaron was away. Lezard was a fine architect but he didn't have the same prestige. Also he had a slight drink problem. Nothing too serious and nothing that yet affected the business. But Aaron knew that the day was coming when he'd have to replace him with someone younger, smarter and cheaper.

Lezard's eyes glinted. 'Do I get to see it, then?'

Aaron sighed an actor's sigh. 'If you really must.' He reached into his briefcase and produced a small box, which was coated in black velvet. A silver button, when pushed, caused the lid to flick open.

Inside lay the golden medal. It rested in a cradle of grey silk. Aaron passed the box over, lid open. 'You can look. But don't touch.'

Lezard grinned. 'Wow. Awesome.'

Aaron caught the faint whiff of malt whisky. He took the medal back. 'Was this why you wanted to see me?'

'No.' Lezard's smile faded. 'While you were away I got rid of Ron Segev. You know, the intern. You remember that thing soon after we took him on? I warned Segev. But it turned out he couldn't let it go.'

'Oh, *that* thing.'

'Exactly. That thing. He just wasn't fitting in. He was upsetting some of the girls. He simply wasn't a team player.'

'Anything in particular?'

'It was the day after you left to get the prize. He turned up with a badge on. You know, that thing again.'

'I comprehend.'

'I know strictly speaking it was your call. But I felt it had to be done. Guys like that are bad for the office and bad for business. Every which way. Can you imagine what a client would think?'

'You did right, Ben. That's absolutely fine. I can't say I'm even the slightest bit surprised. There was something always a bit, I don't know – something not quite right about the guy.'

'There are topics you just don't bring to the office,' Lezard said. 'Especially not *our* office.'

'Exactly,' Aaron agreed.

'Give my love to Esther.'

'Will do.'

'See you Monday, then.'

'Yeah. Sure. You have a great weekend. Bye.'

He went back down to reception to collect his case and then went through the side door and down the concrete steps to the underground car park where he'd left his Merc parked during the trip abroad to collect his prize.

Aaron was forty-five minutes out of the city and had just passed the sign that marked the border with Suffolk. Mercifully, there had been no slow-moving tractors to delay him. He was confident he'd be home by two. Esther wasn't expecting him until eight. It would be a surprise.

Ahead, on a winding section of highway flanked by woodland, a blue Skoda was lingering behind a pair of cyclists with yellow football tops and black ballerina tights who were riding alongside each other. Aaron felt his pulse quicken. Why the hell were these clowns cycling like this on an 'A' road? And what was the zombie in the Skoda up to? Overtake, man! *Jesus!*

If the Skoda wasn't prepared to, he was.

Aaron pressed his foot down hard, taking the pedal to the floor. The Merc surged forward past the inferior machine. He gave the cyclists a blast of the horn to indicate his displeasure at their wilful obstruction of the highway.

It was at this moment that a lunatic came round the bend towards him. Aaron swerved slightly to the left. There was a faint ping as he clipped the nearest cyclist. The ballerina flew off towards the nearest hedgerow as if powered by a jetpack. The frame of the bike followed him like a black vengeful wasp.

The other driver also swerved. They passed with millimetres to spare. Aaron glimpsed the BMW badge. A black face shot past, twisted with rage.

And then it was over. In his rear-view mirror Aaron saw the BMW bounce along the grass verge and regain the highway. Its brake lights came on and it seemed to stop completely.

One of the cyclists was shaking his fist. His companion, miraculously recovered from his brief experience of flight, sprang out of the greenery. He stood in the road, a shrinking figure, as immune from injury as a cartoon character.

Another bend rushed at Aaron. He was well over the white line. Mercifully this time the road was empty.

No harm done, he told himself.

He kept the pedal down until he was near the next roundabout. There he caught up with the inevitable line of cars crawling behind a double-decker bus.

Finally he was round it, and on to the next one, in a familiar sequence. Aaron glanced in his mirror, seeking confirmation of an earlier prickling suspicion. Behind him was a white Fiat Uno, behind that a scarlet Yaris, then a pick-up truck, a white van, another white van. And then a black BMW. It was probably just a coincidence. All the same...

He took the turn to the right and threaded his way past an industrial estate, two supermarkets and a station. He knew the route. A few deft short cuts and he was confident he was not being followed by a vengeful driver.

Gould glanced at the dashboard clock. He still had hours to spare.

On that final stretch of narrow, winding country lane before he met the coast road he spotted an object in the road ahead. As he slowed he saw that it was an animal. It was a rabbit, an extraordinarily small one, barely bigger than a mouse. It was motionless and seemed to be squatting on its haunches. Gould released the brake pedal and drove on, hearing a faint thump beneath him.

Oddly, just minutes later, he saw a second rabbit. It was standing, stiff with terror, on one of the hyphens in the carriageway's white lining. He missed it by a good half metre. The creature was very visibly rigid with fear.

It was his day for noticing members of the Leporidae family. In the next field what at first Aaron thought was a running dog turned out to be an extraordinarily large hare. It shot across the grass some fifty metres to the right of him as if racing his Merc.

And then his attention was wrenched away by the headlights in his rear-view mirror.

It was the BMW. *The* BMW. The silhouette of just one person in the car – an unidentifiable outline of the driver behind the dark glass. The BMW was so close it seemed to float above Aaron's rear window.

A moment later he reached the main road. It was a fast stretch of highway and cars were approaching from both directions but he took a chance. The driver in the nearest lane put on his headlights and pressed his horn down hard. Aaron made it to the far side without being T-boned. He swerved right. The driver coming up behind him also blew his horn – a long unending angry sound.

But he'd made it. In his rear-view mirror he saw that the BMW was still trapped in the side road. The traffic was heavy in both directions.

He overtook three cars, then saw the road ahead was clear. He accelerated to 80.

The attack came without warning, in Jane Austen country.

He was passing a sizeable meadow crowded with grazing sheep when the thick, rippling wave descended. The sheep dissolved, along with the broad expanse of grassland and its scattered oaks. A glimpsed distant, sizeable country house cracked and shattered.

A great chunk of Aaron's vision went.

A piercing pain behind his eyes began to expand its fire towards the base of his neck.

In what was left of his sight a green gap appeared in the

hedgerow beside the road. Vision now almost entirely gone, he steered towards it.

The ground was ribbed with tractor marks. Passing through the gap the car began to shake. Half a dozen symbols on the dashboard came alive with scarlet urgency.

The Merc slewed and slithered and thumped along the field side of the hedgerow

When the shuddering vehicle finally came to a stop Aaron tipped his head forward and closed his eyes. His breath came in quick rasping spurts, like an anguished asthmatic's.

He lived for two or three minutes with the pain and the bright throbbing darkness which danced with jagged grey flakes. Glowing lava poured and bubbled behind the whirling shapes.

He found the red tombstone-shaped migraine relief pill which he always kept tucked in a pocket of his wallet. Eyes closed, he felt for the water bottle resting in its circular nest behind the gear stick. He wrenched the pill from its protective membrane and slipped it into his mouth, swallowing it down with a gulp of warm water. The water had a stale unpleasant taste. He followed it with a pair of paracetamol tablets. They left a gritty taste on his tongue.

The clock on the dashboard confirmed that it was thirteen minutes past noon. Aaron reclined his seat. He closed his eyes and let the pulsing red grid below the closed lids burn itself out. He waited for the medication to kick in.

At some point he fell asleep.

He was trapped alone inside a submarine on the bed of the ocean. The power had failed and there was total blackness.

Something was trying to break in. He felt utter terror.

Thumping noises echoed along the hull.

Aaron woke. There was sweat across his chest and face. He felt cold and shivery. Oddly, he could still hear that ominous thumping.

A hideous satanic face stared at him through the side window. His heart jolted even as he recognised the curling horns as belonging to a sheep.

There were several of them, grouped companionably around the

Merc. As they chomped the grass the group leader's horns banged intermittently against the driver's door.

Aaron sent the window sliding down. He shouted 'Shoo!' and clapped his hands. The sheep scattered.

He hoped the door panel wasn't scratched. If it was he'd eat more lamb. Lots of it.

Aaron saw that the sunlight had gone. Now it was evening.

He'd slept through the entire afternoon. Travel fatigue plus the pills, he guessed. He glanced at the dashboard clock. Perfect. He'd be back at the time he was expected.

A velvet dusk was thickening between the oaks. Isolated members of the distant flock looked like mysterious water creatures in a lake of lavender mist. Aaron farted, then put the car into reverse.

Mercifully, the tyres had a good grip on the muddy, uneven ground. He bumped his way back out of the meadow and rejoined the main road.

The sky was darkening by the minute. The trees at the roadside seemed black and impenetrable. Every vehicle had its lights on.

Aaron drove through Wrentham and soon afterwards passed the side road to Wangford. The church in this last village was where Stanley Spencer had married Hilda Carline.

Sarah had adored Spencer's work. Aaron did not, except for the nudes. She once said Spencer had given her the idea for night architecture. It was the duality of his style during the mid-1920s. Spencer did straightforward landscapes – 'Panorama, Wangford Marsh', 'Stinging Nettles', 'The Red House, Wangford', 'Tree and Chicken Coops' – but at the same time he produced his weird, visionary canvas 'The Resurrection, Cookham'. Inside the ordinary there was always the potential for a re-ordering, a rebirth, a transfiguration. The same applied to buildings. It was a question of how light was arranged.

Sarah had dragged him to Wangford to see the church, which he had found plain and dull. He really only remembered two vivid moments of that trip. One was Sarah exclaiming with delight at a massive clump of nettles at the back of the graveyard, which she proclaimed as Spencerian. The second was fucking her behind the altar and how their echoing cries of pleasure had filled the cold wide space above them like something a passing troupe of angels might have produced.

He had never been back to that place. That was one of his life rules. Never go back. Never try to reproduce what once existed. Never linger with ghosts. Move on, find new people, and make something fresh.

He left Wangford behind and passed among the woodland bordering the sprawling Henham estate. Soon he came to the Blyth estuary. It was high tide and the great expanse of water beside the A12 might easily have been mistaken for the sea. One day – perhaps twenty or thirty years from now – the risen ocean would break through the coastal dunes and the low sandy cliffs. The high salt surge would push its way across the marshes and sweep away this stretch of road. Southwold would become an island and the A12 would require a bridge at this point. Not that Aaron was all that perturbed by this probability. He planned to sell Serena Lodge in a few years and buy an estate in the Scottish highlands.

On he went.

A much superior ecclesiastical structure was this one on the far side of the road as he approached Blythburgh. It protruded like a ship anchored along the low ridge at the eastern tip of the village.

An almost-full moon was low in the sky and in its cold light this ancient flint church at the edge of the marshes looked like the illustration to a ghost story. It stood there, stark and prominent in its outline, mysteriously desolate, framed by the dead and their lichen-spotted memorials.

Soon it dropped away behind some trees.

As he approached The White Hart an automated sign lit up – a red scowling cartoon face above the record of his speed: 55 in a 30 zone.

Aaron slowed to 40, then lower. Just after the pub he peeled off the main road. He went through Blythburgh and reached the crossroads by the water tower, where he took the Walberswick road. Now he was almost home.

He passed the bare acres of the malodorous pig farm and the tree-fringed lay-by which was reputedly favoured by doggers. Soon the road was enveloped by pine woods.

Ahead, on full beam, he saw the line of posts with reflective scarlet lights. They led up to a pair of conifers which flanked the five-bar gate across the entrance to a narrow single-track drive. PRIVATE it said on the gate, which swung open automatically as Aaron approached.

He turned into the drive, where the word PRIVATE echoed along the silver birches lining the route.

At first, Esther had not wanted to live here. The thought of being sometimes alone in this large house in such an isolated location made her nervous. She had once had a boyfriend who liked horror films. From his enthusiasm she had learned what happens to attractive young women who find themselves on their own in a forest at night. Especially when the locals are subnormal.

Suffolk might not be Louisiana but you only had to look at who its MPs were to know that this was a seriously backward region.

Aaron smoothed her fears away. Their home was protected by a high perimeter fence, reinforced by a thick holly hedge. There were sensors and a surveillance system. The security was sophisticated and cutting edge.

Serena Lodge even had a panic room, though this was never mentioned to journalists.

Aaron encouraged her to have lots of girlfriends to stay. He reminded her that she was living in one of the safest parts of the country, with a near-zero crime rate. The last recorded local offence was the pilfering of the dog bowl outside the delicatessen in Walberswick. Plus in nearby Southwold there had been a brawl in The Red Lion involving a pair of tattooed female proles, resulting in a bloodied nose. That was it.

The absence of criminality required substitute anxieties, which were supplied in the form of local legends. Black Shuck, the devil's dog, which scorched church doors. An alien spacecraft seen hovering over Rendlesham Forest. A sea monster glimpsed off

Kessingland. A strange creature seen slumbering among the reeds of the River Deben. Nonsense like that.

The lane curved through woodland and almost at once reached a tall wide gate of black wrought iron set in a pair of brick columns. To one side was a secure structure with flaps for mail and parcel deliveries, as well as a turning space. This was the furthest limit for an unsolicited visit by a member of the service class.

As Aaron approached the gate slid open to admit the Mercedes.

Beyond it the drive dipped sharply down into a tunnel. Lights embedded in the walls flickered on as the car entered. A sequence of small, discreet CCTV cameras tracked his route to the house.

The tunnel still rankled. It was the price Aaron had had to pay for the planners' refusal to extinguish the public footpath along the old railway line.

He emerged into Serena Lodge's parking area, which was unexpectedly generous. An existing quarry had been widened and deepened to create it. Parking for twenty cars. Invisible from the surrounding woodland; a planner's delight.

From the base of the modernised quarry – most of its walls had been rendered under sheets of concrete but some of the original rock surface had been retained under a fine metal mesh – a stylish metal staircase looped round, curling upward to the house. The prize-wining structure could not be seen until you reached the quarry's lip.

In the north-facing side of the quarry two metal doors accessed a further parking area, built deep under the Lodge. One of the doors slid upward and Aaron drove into his personal bay. The place had the coldness of all underground parking but an attempt had been made to humanise this bleak space with bright paintwork, extra lighting, and plants that thrived in the dim glow projected from concealed light-wells. 'Amazing,' the reporter from *The Sunday Times* had asserted when shown it, before going on to describe Aaron as 'craggily handsome' and blessed with 'a quietly commanding presence'.

Aaron had later met up with scarlet-haired-and-toed Martina Jekyll for a number of memorable afternoons at a hotel in the City, before they decided to call it a day. Marriage is not to be entered into unadvisedly or lightly, but reverently, deliberately, and in accordance with the purposes for which it was instituted by God, she had whispered, riding him, interspersed with cries of shit, fuck and (wittily reciting James Joyce) yes oh yes. Sweet hot memories, rising with him as he stepped back outside, having turned away from the elevator to the house, honouring his phobia. He'd pressed the button – but only to put his suitcase in the infernal device, sending it on its way for collection later.

Up he went, gripping the banister, mounting the metal stairwell as it followed the quarry's flanks. Rooks fluttered and fidgeted in the adjacent woodland, emitting a few harsh metallic cries. It was a warm smooth evening, the last patches of indigo sky giving way to a sprinkling of stars.

He continued on up the steps.

Somewhere further off a bird of night screamed a sequence of brief mournful farewells to the extinguished day. Aaron farted explosively and the birdsong stopped.

Dutch food, he thought. Was it the wild Beemster duck or the caramelized Jonagold apples? Perhaps the chemical interaction of both dishes being broken down in his guts? Whatever it was he felt full of wind. It was good to rid his body of it out before he encountered Esther.

Panting slightly, he reached the top. Serena Lodge did not so much come into view as appear slowly to assemble itself from its surroundings. Long horizontal strips of timbered façade seemed to *glow* into existence, bringing to life tall slender windows like enlarged slits for archers defending an ancient castle. The building gradually took shape as an assemblage of sculpted fragments – 'a giant Georges Braque canvas come to life in rural Suffolk!' as Martina Jekyll had described it to her half-million adoring followers. Each fragment began to take precedence in turn until at last they dimmed, bringing into prominence the ramp leading up to the great double-doored entrance. Here, the homage to Mayan architecture was obvious. ('No one does kitsch quite like Aaron Gould,' the left-wing art critic Jan Borger had sarcastically remarked – that stung but Aaron strongly suspected the motive was primarily political rather than aesthetic.)

These effects were all part of the mechanics of night architecture. The observer, arriving at nightfall and reaching the top of the quarry ('A simply stunning metaphor for that void from which we all emerge and to which we inevitably return' – Martina Jekyll), found herself dazzled by banks of lights. They cut out, plunging the observer into darkness. Then the magic began: the illumination in turn of different aspects of the fabric, while twinkling lights marked the limits of the path that led towards the Lodge entrance. On special occasions piped music wafted the top ten tunes from the Classic FM playlist.

By the time the visitor drew close the Lodge had taken shape as a dark corrugated mass. Reaching the end of the path you became aware of terraced troughs of wildflowers, speckling the frontage with dots of yellow and purple. Two stray poppies looked like observant eyes. 'Aaron Gould is passionate about the environment and each delicate petal is a tribute to that commitment' – Martina Jekyll in her quasi-purple profile.

The crest of the house was capped by silver toadstools – vents for the log burning stoves and other heating accoutrements required by an awareness of the useful Green Housing Awards which eco-design could scoop up. Serena Lodge had won six.

The house responded to the proximity of Aaron's phone, opening one of its doors to let him in. 'Welcome home, Aaron,' Stanley the hallway robot said, rolling towards him and raising its stiff arms to take his umbrella.

Esther did not like the robot and had urged him to dispose of it but the device charmed and amused visitors. 'Oh my God it's so *adorable!*' Martina had cried, on seeing the machine. 'It's so damn cute I want to *fuck* it!' And to Aaron's surprise and then deepening anxiety – Esther was somewhere upstairs in the house – Martina slipped off her skirt and knickers and pressed her skinny thighs around the robot's head. She moved energetically to and fro until she noisily climaxed.

Both at the time and later Aaron never could decide whether her orgasm was genuine or performative. But then again he'd had the same thought on the twenty-seven occasions when he'd fucked her.

'Umbrella, Aaron,' Stanley chided him, as he walked past and through the door, closing it behind him.

He heard the robot's rubber fists bumping against the door, still seeking an absent umbrella. Then it gave up. 'Goodbye, Aaron. See you around.'

Aaron did not reply. Never reply to a robot, unless issuing a command. It will only seek to prolong the conversation.

He went on up two flights of steps to the top floor where he knew he'd find Esther. She'd either be resting in bed, in the kitchen fixing his evening meal, or in the living room.

It was good to be home. Here he felt safe from everything. As he went up to her he passed the gallery of pictures displayed along the wall. He'd picked up the idea from a visit to Kipling Manor. Mick and Delphine Owen – two of the most delightful people in English society. Their country home was less than half an hour's drive away. Aaron was flattered to learn that Mick had read and admired *Night Architecture*. He'd always been a huge Mick Owen fan. Apart from their genius they discovered they had much in common when it came to politics.

Now, breathing heavily, Aaron ascended to the point where the wall displayed the framed photograph of them together: the major novelist and the great architect, both a little younger, possibly just a little slimmer, with maybe more and darker hair. They each looked slightly startled, turning to stare at the photographer, their half-emptied flutes clutched at a semi-detumescent angle within their fists.

A Louis Blore image. Louis had long ago become the new David Bailey – the photographer celebrities wanted. Louis liked spontaneity. His pics had an authenticity which more considered compositions lacked. He favoured the tousled, the windswept, the surprised. He liked to make his subjects jump. They adored his jests. When Louis was around with his little cheap Canon – the artistry came later, the image cropped, twisted, adjusted for colour and shade – they knew *something* would happen to surprise them. Startled, a little dishevelled, they grinned. It made these greed monsters seem human, even *ordinary*. Torn jeans, ripped skirts, patched clothing – the prole look was currently the quintessence of chic. It hid the wealth and the moral hollow.

Louis was great with kids, too – a bit of a clown, exuberant, funny-face-puller, adept at Irish and Scottish accents. As well as Brooklyn and Texas. In short, an absolute hoot.

Upstairs Aaron could hear music playing. Maybe it was Grieg. Whatever it was it sounded Nordic. Full-blooded orchestral melancholy, evoking vast pine forests and fjords flanked by mountains. And inside his head an intermittent voice, not his, he felt. Odd. Perhaps he needed a test.

He continued on, more slowly now, to the top floor.

It always felt slightly strange returning to this place.

He'd first come here to this woodland bordering the Blyth marshland with Sarah. It was not long after they'd become lovers. How long ago all that seemed, now. Another lifetime. It was Sarah, a fellow architecture student, who'd educated him about painting – and other things, including Suffolk, her home county. Back then this place was wilderness – a secret place close to an ancient heronry. George Orwell made love to a Southwold girl in these woods, she told him, unhooking her black bra. Sarah was sophisticated, clever, extraordinarily beautiful, unbelievably sexy.

He was glad he'd built Serena Lodge in this place. It felt like a triumphal arch erected after a great victory.

In those days he was an obscure architecture student – bright, driven, but lacking in originality. It was Sarah who had the ideas, the feel for form, the vision of fresh possibilities. She'd drafted an essay on the use of lighting to reverse the daytime appearance of a building: 'The Architecture of Night'. It had both dazzled and embittered him. She saw things he'd never thought of. Brilliance in a woman is unnerving and although he was proud she was *his*, he resented her. He could see far into the future: she would be the star, he would be the biological appendage. People would be charming to him but only because he was *her* favourite. Leonard was right. That's how it goes. And everybody knows.

'Have you shown this to anyone?'

'Only you.'

'It's stunning.'

'Yes, it is rather good, isn't it? Innovative. I'm amazed no one ever thought of it before.' Her eyes were merry. 'But then the profession has always been dominated by men.'

'We have other uses,' he said, tugging at the belt of her skirt.

'Beast!'

'You bet.'

Yes, in those days they couldn't keep their hands off each other. Sex at dawn, sex in the afternoon, sex at midnight. Strange how little of it he remembered, now. Sex blurs. His past was a mist of embraces, few of which lingered with the precision of a photograph. Mary with the spiky red hair he remembered, riding him, her big breasts swaying. Black-haired Gina, grinning up at him, his semen trickling down her chin. With Sarah he recalled fucking in woods and fields and on beaches, but there was little in the way of detail. And what he remembered most of all in the end wasn't the sex but the end of the affair. That morning – that dark day. Deep down he would never be free of it.

Sarah went off to make breakfast. He dozed on their inflatable bed. It always had a faint wobble, as if it was afloat on a lake rippled by a mild breeze.

Aaron heard the whistle of the scarlet kettle on the hob, the clang of a pan. She returned to the bedroom of their tiny top floor apartment in Shoreditch, naked. Sarah had always liked to walk around naked. There were tall buildings nearby, anyone staring at their apartment would surely see. 'Let them,' she'd say. 'Give the five-fingered-widow brigade a treat.' There was an exhibitionist inside her, he realised, which added to her inventory of thrilling characteristics. She preferred fucking outdoors, where there was a faint risk of someone seeing them.

'Scrambled eggs on toast for the master, with black coffee,' Sarah said dryly, with that little half-smile he'd always remember. And then her face changed, utterly. Her forehead and her cheeks turned a beetroot colour. The beetroot flush instantly drained away and she became entirely grey. She stared at him, her mouth becoming oddly twisted, as if she was struggling to say something. And then her eyes flicked shut and she dropped lifeless to the ground, crashing across shattered breakfast plates and a sludge of egg yolk.

This was back in the days when if you called for an ambulance one came within ten minutes. By this time he'd managed to wipe off the egg and get her nude body inside her dressing gown. He hurriedly dressed. Sarah looked dead but she wasn't – he felt her pulse. It was faint but it was there.

Aaron had no idea what had happened. Had she being doing drugs and not telling him? They didn't do drugs, ever. Sarah liked cocktails and fine wine; Aaron too. He was baffled. A stroke? But strokes only happened to fat people and the elderly, didn't they?

Astonishingly, Sarah's green eyes opened as the crew arrived. She stared at Aaron but without recognition. What the fuck had *happened*?

They lifted her into a wheelchair, and then her eyes closed again and her head slumped forwards, chin hard against her clavicle.

It was a brain haemorrhage. Sarah had been born with a condition inside her head which was basically like an explosive fixed to a timer. The bomb duly detonated at its appointed time. She lingered on in hospital for three days and then died.

After the funeral her father drew him aside. 'I always liked you, Aaron. I thought one day you'd be our son-in-law. But now she's gone Karen and I don't ever want to see you again. It's nothing personal, you understand. You are young. You'll find someone new. I understand. You can move on from what's happened but we never can. And your presence in our life would be too painful because of that.'

'But Mr Aaronovitch –'

Sarah's father cut in. 'Please, Aaron. No words, I beg you. I know you are hurting. But that hurt will fade, in time. Ours never will. Spare me the greetings card sentiments.'

Silence.

And then he produced a grey Baddeley Brothers envelope. 'This is for you. No – don't open it now. And when you do please don't get in touch with me. I don't need to hear your thanks.'

Aaron took it and folded it into his wallet.

'I'm doing this for Sarah. I know she'd want me to help you on your way with your career. I'm sure you'll make a fine architect. You could get there on your own, I know. But money always helps.'

With a brief pat to Aaron's shoulder he was gone.

Opening the envelope back at the apartment – the lease ran for another eight months and despite its ever-present ghost Aaron didn't feel inclined to leave – he looked at the figure on the Coutts cheque. *Half a million pounds.*

There is nothing quite as sweet in life as the unexpected acquisition of a very large sum of money. Aaron sometimes pondered if it wasn't even better than sex. On the whole he thought it was.

He invested this stupendous gift in property. A sideline. In retrospect that was a very smart decision. A few tricks of the architectural trade and he was soon tripling what he'd paid for a house. This was the golden age of property speculation. Awesome.

Esther rose a little unsteadily from the armchair. She picked up her phone and muted the orchestra. 'I've missed you so much!'

'And I've missed you.'

Aaron moved towards her and took her in his arms. 'I hated having to leave you so close to the birth.'

'It was important you went.'

He leaned forwards over the great swelling to embrace her. A lingering hug, a long kiss. Her belly pressed against him. She seemed enormous. Like a figure in a cartoon enlarged by an air pressure pump.

But soon she would pop and collapse back to her usual dimensions (well he hoped so – he didn't want a fat wife).

Aaron was glad it was going to be a boy. There was so much less to worry about. Plus he'd have an heir. His breed would endure.

They were calling the child Samuel, after her father. Aaron got on well with his father-in-law, but it never hurt to flatter. Esther, fortunately, was an only child. The apple of, etcetera.

Her father, Sam Cohen, was the stratospherically wealthy owner of HBS, a components supplier. If people knew about the company at all they usually confused it with a bank. Samuel was a Dickens character. A charming man – big, bearded, the paunch of a well-fed and successful individual who was at home with himself and with the world. There was a distinct resemblance to the current Chief Rabbi.

Samuel Cohen's shining world became Aaron's world too. And he said to himself how wonderful it was. So much more pleasant than that grey sphere inhabited by a large peevish population whose primary mode of communication was complaint.

'Poor you,' she breathed and for a moment he was perplexed. Aaron was a fortunate and accomplished individual, in need of no one's sympathy. But when she raised a hand and pressed the tips of her fingers to his brow he realised she meant his migraine attack. In telling his tale – it was a much abbreviated version of that drive from Norwich – his mind had briefly wandered away to a small anxiety. Had the police called? he wondered. He did not phrase it like that. Instead he asked if she'd had any visitors today. No, none. Aaron relaxed a little.

And then in the silence he heard somewhere on the floor below a distant toilet flush, followed by the faint sound of a door shutting.

'Is someone else here?'

'Relax.' Esther smiled. 'It's only George.'

'George?'

'One of the gardeners. He's been working late on the primroses in the troughs on the east side of the house. I said he could use one of the toilets downstairs.'

'I don't think I've met George.'

'Emma couldn't come today. She's not well. George is her replacement. He seems quite sweet.'

'Handsome?'

Esther grinned. 'Totally.' She gave him a playful poke. 'Jealous, are we?'

'Insanely.'

He glanced at his phone. It had a link to the house CCTV. Aaron watched George come out of the house and then turn right into an area of darkness. He swiftly emerged from it pushing a bicycle. Aaron zoomed in. Bearded, longish hair, slim. Looked to be about thirty.

George mounted his bike and rode off into the exit tunnel. The pinprick of his rear light disappeared from view. Aaron put the phone down. 'It's completely gone. I feel fine now. I'm as right as rain. I don't know what came over me.'

Aaron did not like his dialogue. It was marriage dialogue. It was the price you paid. At least his second attachment was a success.

By now he had produced the bauble which had taken him away. Esther held the medal in her hand and touched it cautiously, as if it might fracture or burst.

'My genius,' she said proudly, squeezing his hand.

'I couldn't have done it without you,' he said.

More marriage dialogue. It went with the genre. If he hadn't become an architect he would surely have found employment as a highly successful writer of screenplays.

'Nonsense!' she said gaily.

CU: Gives her a tender look. 'I mean it.' He reaches out and rests his hand on her –

It didn't – it doesn't – get any better. Coochy-coochy-coo would follow, he felt certain. But that was as yet a matter for the imagination.

Her conversation faded as Aaron went elsewhere, by smooth electric scooter. Esther chattered brightly on, telling him about Lulu's phone call and what Lulu had told her about her cousin Cynthia, who had a baby, who was named Rosie. The amazing thing about Cynthia –

Aaron's mind had wheeled back to his first marriage. The Catastrophe, as he privately called it.

Edith had bewitched him. She wasn't even his type – too tall, too gaunt, too angular. Skinny. Aaron liked meat on a woman. Edith lacked much in the way of a rump. Her breasts were tiny, yet they drooped. He could still see them in his mind's bedroom archive (as well as in certain files kept in a subterranean region of his tablet). They were strangely pointed. But none of that seemed to matter at the time. Aaron's tastes were broad. He wasn't fixated on size. The right kind of human stick insect could be as pleasurable as a whale.

What caught his attention was her understanding of desire. She knew bedways – and how... Gee whiz! Crikey! Fireworks rising beyond the Sydney Opera House!

Edith introduced him to tricks he didn't know about or had never tried. It was sex that sealed their union. There was nothing she wouldn't do. Intoxicated by pleasure he decided he couldn't afford to let a woman like that slip through his sticky fingers...

Admittedly there was her older brother, Dave. Dave made little attempt to mask his hostility towards the new boyfriend. He plainly resented Aaron for his wealth, his accomplishments, his success. Poor Dave. He repaired guitars and drove a Ford Fiesta. His conversation at its best concerned obscure keyboard bands of the 1990s but mainly it consisted of gibes, whinges and broad-spectrum sundry negativities.

'So Cynthia said –'

But Dave was in Camden and the newly married Goulds had removed themselves to their new home in Tasburgh. That was a mistake. Edith was bored by village life. In their beginning was their end. A greasy mechanic in oil-stained overalls, little more than a teenager, occupied her time during his business absences. It took a while to learn of this development.

Aaron shut down the memories. Enough back story; enough flashbacks. Live for the moment...

'And now Philip is divorcing her!'

Esther stared at him, expecting a response.

'Goodness. That's a bit of a shock.'

He tried to remember who Philip was, and failed.

Next, she began to describe at length, as if seeking to persuade a jury, how Cynthia's friend Mary was locked in a protracted dispute over a really, really unfair parking ticket.

It was one of those hyper-real star-spangled VVG nights.

They sat on the terrace gazing out over the grey expanse of Angel Marsh, beneath a sky criss-crossed by belts of incandescent balls of gas. The firmament was so bright you suspected it had been rigged up by an electrician from the special effects department.

Stars are born from clouds of dust, just as nostalgia for bright lost love is. Aaron realised that had his fate forked in a quite different direction he would have excelled in the greetings card business. Gould's Cards for People Who Care about Life. Gould's Cards for People Who Care about Meaning. Gould's Cards for Word People with Hearts. He wouldn't have needed any help from Don Draper.

Esther sipped her iced mineral water.

Aaron poured himself a third glass of Pinot Noir.

The lamb casserole with rice and salad had been wonderful.

Faraway, on the opposite side of the estuary, pairs of tiny white eyes appeared from time to time in the darkness. Cars, moving in and out of Southwold. The lighthouse couldn't be seen from the house but over to the north-east a faint pulsing glimmer above the conifers indicated its turning beam.

Aaron rested his hand on Esther's inner thigh. 'I've missed you in more ways than one,' he smiled.

It was their secret code. She grinned. 'You're incorrigible.' And then: 'Where would you like me to be?'

'Are you joining in?'

'Not tonight, my emperor.'

'In that case...'

At one end of the terrace, under a projecting slice of roof, a pair of wickerwork sofas and big cushion-filled armchairs were grouped around a large coffee table.

Esther positioned herself naked at the edge of one of the armchairs. Her vast belly resembled a smooth rock encountered while ascending a green bare mountain slope. That memorable one near Swordland Lodge, for example.

Aaron tilted his body, releasing a silent gush of sulphur into the night air.

He stood before his wife, then bent his knees and lowered himself far enough to penetrate her while remaining standing.

Esther was dry, tight, and winced as he pushed into her. That was good, it increased the pressure on his penis. Her response excited him.

He came very quickly.

When his penis started to shrink he pulled out of her and sank to the ground on his knees. He leaned forward and rested the side of his face against her spectacular mass of jet-black pubic hair. He had never known a woman quite so hairy down there (except once, in Brazil).

Esther stroked his head. 'Satisfied, my emperor?'

'Mmmmmmm.'

Ten minutes later she was in bed. Aaron had a quick shower and joined her. He glanced at his phone. *The latest economic statement from – The Prime Minister has said that – In Wales the tragic case of –*

An Atlantic storm was heading for County Galway.

In East Anglia a light frost was forecast.

Aaron put his phone on mute and turned out the light.

Part Two

Shhhh says the German Ocean. *Shhhh* says the North Atlantic. *Pish* says the hairy Scot. The griddle pumps are broken! What does this mean? It means nothing. Where does this information come from? It comes from the interstices. *Pish* says the hairy Scot. *Shhhh* says the tiny yellow can of Schweppes tonic water. The hairy Scot. He was the first James Bond. The hairy Scot is dressed in a pleated kilt, with long leather boots. His matted chest is exposed. A leather belt, like the support for a guitar, is slung between his nipples. *Dance*, cries Mozart. *Mourn*, mutters Beethoven. *Engine pulp*, whirrs the handheld silver whisk. And now you can hear playing across the wilderness of marsh and moor the second movement of the Seventh Symphony. O'Hara grew up believing he had been born in June, but in fact had been born in March, his parents having disguised his true date of birth because he was conceived out of wedlock. *While I have certain regrets, I am still glad I got there before Alain Robbe-Grillet did.* On it goes, drawling and lyrical, that second movement of the Seventh Symphony. *Pish* says the hairy Scot. Now I am quietly waiting for – Aaron passes on through the scenery and its voices. He may be some kind of butterfly. He appears to be in flight, but jerkily. See! A bright successive nonsense fabric. Here, a dark-haired woman fingers a guitar. Here, a sign reads: DO NOT BE LATE FOR THE FUNICULAR. Here, a giant ice-cream cornet drips. A 99, with a flake. A scream rips through it all. Aaron is jolted awake. He can still hear the scream even though there is now only silence. It repeats in his head. He looks at his bedside clock. 1.20am. Aaron lies there and attempts to decipher the scream's meaning. Was it in his dream? Or was it simply the strange cry of a bird in the night? Just occasionally, close to the house, something disturbs a rook or a crow. You hear them fluttering in the depths of the highest branches. Sometimes they shoot out from their roosts with a bloodcurdling half-human sound. Or perhaps a screech-owl. There are other rational explanations. Foxes reside in these woods. Their cries can sometimes seem human. Twice – which in the context of their time here makes it a rare occurrence – a territorial stag in rut has stood by the perimeter fence and articulated its hot, roaring, full-throated male presence. Aaron lies there, listening to the fast beat of his pulse. He can feel the blood-throb just above and behind his ears. As the source of the scream Black Shuck can be ruled out. The knowledgeable guide who'd showed them round Holy Trinity at Blythburgh had scotched that myth. Indicating the supposed scorch marks on the ancient wooden door the man had dryly explained that this medieval legend was unknown before the 1950s. As for the rings attached to the great stone columns, they were not used by Cromwell's men to tether horses but put there in the nineteenth century in order to chain-up the oil-fired heaters, which villagers kept stealing. Only Aaron and Esther had turned up for the tour. The man, a genial guy with a dry sense of humour, had evidently taken a shine to them. When the tour was over he invited them back to his home in the village for coffee. It was coffee that would have passed the David Lynch test. And on a wall in the living room hung a painting, hidden behind a canvas-sized curtain, by a woman artist of some reputation. Their host, whose name Aaron could no longer remember, had been proud of his possession. Understandably. The painter – whose name Aaron also could now no longer remember – was familiar to him from her painting in the National Gallery (or was it Tate Britain?). The one of the artist reflected in a full-length mirror as she painted a nude woman. Aaron had remembered it particularly for that pert nude ass. He was a connoisseur of the naked female form and that painting captured his interest. That this church guy owned a painting by the same painter was impressive. Aaron wondered how much it had cost to buy and what it was currently worth. Paintings and first editions are both excellent investments. There are a few Maggi Hamblings around Serena Lodge, along with two small canvases by George Frederick Watts and an early sketch by

Lucien Freud. Plus seven Carol Wyatts... Aaron lies there, alert, listening. The atmosphere in the bedroom seems unpleasantly hot and sticky. His chest is coated in a cold sweat. Has the air-conditioning unit malfunctioned? But now there's a sudden low roar as the machinery comes alive, pumping gusts of cool air into the room. He recalls closing the window. Unlikely to have been a bird, then. Beside him, the big heavy lump of female flesh that is Esther stirs and emits a sequence of small, quick snorts. She smells buttery in the darkness. Buttery, with a faint hint of cream past its sell-by date. He feels a familiar pressure on his bladder. It's the price you pay for growing old, for drinking too much, too late. Aaron rolls out of bed and pads naked to the door. He always sleeps in the nude. In the bedroom's grey light his erection, at half mast, points the way. He could piss in the en-suite but he doesn't want to wake Esther. Very gently he twists the handle, then closes the door behind him. Seconds later dim lighting comes alive in the corridor. Aaron heads for the stairs and walks down to the next floor, where there are eight guest bedrooms. He enters the nearest one and goes to its en-suite to urinate. Returning to the corridor he pauses, listening. He's been thinking about that scream. He's decided it probably came from one of the floors below. It might just be a trick of the acoustics. Serena Lodge has echoes he hadn't anticipated when he designed it. He puts it down to the lack of carpeting in the lower floors. He walks down to the next floor and stands in the dim light. His pulse starts to speed up again as he hears something. Not a scream but a whimpering. A faint but sustained ejaculation of distress, as from a hurt animal. It lasts for a good sixty seconds before it cuts out. Then only silence, apart from the thudding of his veins. Next the air con starts up again, humming as it blasts Aaron Gould's face with a sudden icy breeze. This is distinctly odd. Troubling, even. It sounds like *something* down there. Yet the house security is sophisticated and surely cannot have been breached. Not unless that damn fool gardener left a door open and something slipped in. A squirrel? A cat? He descends to the next floor, hearing nothing but the rhythms of the air conditioning. Then the cold air pauses with a click and in the lengthening silence the whimpering begins again. The floor below, unquestionably. That utilitarian zone where the washing machines and tumble dryers are located. Though it sounds like a small child, he guesses it must be a cat. Perhaps even a fluffy, lost kitten. Did it sneak in after him when he drove into the garage? Aaron descends to this final floor. There's no air conditioning here – just functional minimalism. The corridor floor is uncarpeted. He feels a small physical shock as the soles of his feet encounter cold slate tiles. He stands at the foot of the stairwell, staring down the corridor. There are four doors on either side. One, at the far end on the right, is half-open. This is where the whimpering is coming from. He pushes the door fully open and quickly reaches in and flicks the light switch on the left. The fluorescent tubes crackle momentarily then flood the room with light. Aaron enters. The room, some five metres wide by twenty deep, is bare and empty. Windowless and underground, it was designed as a storage room. The walls are unplastered brick, the floor rough concrete with a pattern of tiny serrations. In the end the house contained so much storage space that this room was never needed. As he glances in all he sees is a fridge-freezer-size filing cabinet, blood red in colour, standing in the corner on the far right. He remembers now. It used to be in his study but the advent of digital storage rendered its bulky presence unnecessary. It was demoted to this storage room on the off-chance that one day it might be needed again. But it never has been. Beside the filing cabinet someone – one of the gardeners, presumably – has placed a spade. Its silver blade has a few crumbs of earth clinging to it. Apart from these two objects the room is entirely empty. Nothing can be hiding behind the filing cabinet, because it's wedged into the corner. Did the noise come from *inside* it? A trapped kitten? Highly unlikely – but there's only one way to tell. As he sets out across the room to look the lights above him make a fluttering sound and begin to flicker. The sound reminds him of a big frantic moth beating its wings against the inside of a lampshade. Aaron sees that the ends of the trio of long slender bulbs are seamed with dark patches like a cancer X-ray. They need replacing. One of the tubes dies, then a second one. The third one also fails. But as he stops in the darkness they come back to life, offering brief playful scraps of light before finally casting off their flirtation to yield a harsh, overpowering incandescence. It's cold in here and he's naked. He decides he'll take a quick look inside each of the filing cabinet drawers, then go back to bed. It's at this moment, as he approaches the corner, that the door behind him slams abruptly shut. A sharp crash. This rush of sound fills the room, bouncing off the walls, repeating. It makes him jump, decidedly. What *the fuck* is going on? It's like poltergeist activity. Except that everyone knows poltergeist activity is carried out by messed-up teenage girls whose mommy or daddy are having sex with someone who is not their spouse. Plus apart from the Freud thing, said girls are probably itching to get laid. Aaron goes back to the door, opens it, and steps out into the corridor. He looks up and down. Zilch. A puzzle. Doors on this level do not have the automation option. A strong wind blowing through the house? Has Esther opened a window? Sometimes a gale comes in from the North Sea and barrels down the estuary without warning. He'll check the windows when he goes back upstairs. As he stands there he hears it again. A faint whimper, barely more than a whisper. Unquestionably coming from the room he's just left. Aaron goes back in, determined to solve this mystery. He's half way across the room, heading for the filing cabinet – the source of the noise *has* to be in that damn piece of office furniture – when the door slams shut behind him again. The shock of it makes his chest seem to contract. Simultaneously all the lights go out. He pauses, breathing heavily. *What in fuck's name...* Jesus... Aaron stands there, letting his pulse slide back to normal. Getting his breath back. Processing what's occurred. The light failure can be explained. Not that slamming door. A faint prickle of anxiety disturbs his composure. He suddenly feels terribly vulnerable. He's naked. Nothing on his feet, even. Plus he left his phone in the bedroom. It's a hot night but it's cool inside this room of brick and concrete. The tiny ridges of the rough floor are not comfortable to stand on with bare feet. Time to get out of this place. Fuck whatever was making that noise. He'll check it out tomorrow. Bring heavy-duty flashlights. Wedge the door open, replace the fluorescent tubes. And rip that goddam filing cabinet apart. But for now it's time to return to bed. If Esther wakes she'll wonder where he is. Aaron turns round and steps forward cautiously in the pitch dark. Back to the door. He stretches out both arms ahead of him, his fingers spread, reaching for the edge of the door. Waiting for that moment of contact with a hard smooth surface. Six paces, seven, eight... The absence of light is disorientating. Nine, ten, eleven. *Where's that fucking door?* Twelve, thirteen, fourteen. What the – ? Fifteen, sixteen, seventeen. Aaron stops. His pulse is back to a sequence of wild drum-beats filling his chest and his head. He feels a little dizzy. Take a deep breath. Slow your breathing. That's what he learned in yoga. Learn to be calm. The mind is a cage of chattering monkeys. Sedate those wretched agitated creatures with soft thoughts of orange blossom drifting gently across an orchard. Let blue slow waves fall on an empty beach of silver sand. Relax and now empty your mind. He farts, noisily. A thick rich meaty stench seems to fill the room. Where *the fuck* is that door? He walks on. And on. And on. This makes no sense at all. The room is of generous proportions but it's not *that* big. He needs a wall. If he can just get to a wall he can feel his way round to the door. On he goes, the hard rough floor beginning to hurt more, now. *Jesus.* What's happening? It's like the room's *expanded* in some way. Not possible. Get a grip. Stop. Take lots of deep breaths. Try to figure out what's happening. Aaron suddenly understands. It's that black guy. The one in the BMW. He must have seen the Merc behind the hedge. He fixed a tracking device. Then he waited further down the road, just off it, somewhere inconspicuous. The Factory Shop car park in Wrentham, say. Then when he drove past the guy followed, at a distance. He pursued him all the way home. Aaron feels a chill. The guy must be a major league drug dealer. Or a gangster. And now he's out for revenge... Right now he's upstairs doing unspeakable things to Esther. No. Don't be absurd. Get a grip. All the same. *Enemies...* There's quite a list. Could be the guy that Ben fired, Ron, the intern. A troublemaker *and* an architect. But he wouldn't have the resources. Besides, he'd blame Ben, not the boss. Aaron had been out of the country. Also, wouldn't you need Esther's help? No, rule that suspect out,

Inspector. What about all those people who'd objected to the Gould Building in Norwich? Hundreds of them. But that was years ago. And anyway, wouldn't the target be that structure – not the architect at his home several years later? Also, it was only a planning controversy. Not really the kind of thing that required extreme revenge. Plus the protests had come from the flabby petition-signing brigade. They lacked teeth. More of a worry, now he thought about it, were those eco-loons who'd objected to Serena Lodge being built in woodland designated A Site of Special Scientific Interest. The eco whingers. Lovers of foxes, deer and other vermin. Not to mention all those bloody creepy-crawlies which got uprooted, and the hurt feelings among our feathered friends down by the heronry. FFS. Those nutters had been spear-headed by a mad couple, what were their names? Jake somebody. Smythe? Something like that. Plus his whiny Welsh faery queen, Bethan. Dreadlocks, nose piercings, a wispy costume straight out of *Lord of the Rings*. That toxic twosome had attacked the contractor's cabins and a digger. They'd been caught, convicted of criminal damage and arson, and had gone down for eight years. They must be out by now. *Shit*. It *must* be them. It's fucking *Cape Fear* all over again. Aaron is feeling shaky, on edge. No. Dismiss that suspicion. Those bunglers would never get past the security systems. Unless they had an accomplice. Of course. *George*. That fucking new gardener. Bound to be an eco loon himself, on the quiet. Men who garden – it's not normal. But still hard to see how they could pull the slamming door trick. And the absence of walls. Stay where you are. Think hard. Don't move an inch. Keep breathing slowly. Try to figure what this is all about. *Fuck it*. This is all in his head. He's disorientated, that's all. A momentary dizziness. The wine? Aaron decides he's had enough of this crap. He swings round to the right, once again holding out his arms in the dark. He walks ten paces and his fingertips touch nothing. He keeps walking. Nothing. He moves faster. Nothing. He hisses through his teeth with rage and frustration. It's a behavioural tic. Esther has gently brought it to his attention on a number of occasions. She doesn't mind when it's just the two of them. But when others are present... Also his grunts, his sighs, his groans.

As his impatience with the follies of the world grows stronger, so too do his involuntary expulsions of sound. Also his swearing. Esther says it's getting worse and please to stop it. Especially when others are present. Also she does not want their child hearing such language. Babies are sponges and mimics. It might culminate in considerable embarrassment. One thinks of nurseries and crèches. *Fuckit.* This situation is *totally absurd.* He *designed* this goddam room. He watched it all being built, this house. He continues to walk on, touching nothing. Stops again. Try to stay calm. More slow deep breathing. Get rid of the chattering monkeys. Think it through. Esther will wake soon. After a while she'll come looking for him. She will, in the end, check every room in the house. Sooner or later she'll get to the door and open it and the room will flood with light and this will all be over. Stay calm. Drift with that thought. Whatever *the fuck* is happening, help will come. Sooner or later. Sooner or later. Wonder what time it is? Feeling a little colder, now. And all so black. Silence. Minutes pass. Pulse slower now. Back to normal. *Of course!* Now he understands. There's only one person who could have done this. Well, not a person exactly. *Stanley.* Never underestimate the capacity of a robot. Stanley must have hacked into the house systems. It's Stanley who's rigged up the door-slamming trick. It's Stanley who's killed the lights. It's Stanley who's trapped him here. It's AI paranoia come true. Stanley has developed independent thinking and emotions. And Stanley is staging his own slave revolt. It reminds Aaron of a movie he once saw. *The Demon Seed.* Julie Christie in her prime trapped inside her home by a computer which wants her to bear its child. So, nothing personal, then. Stanley just wants to have Esther and all that stands in his way is Aaron. Unless of course Stanley has already had his way with Esther and that foetus inside her belly is not Aaron's... *Stop it!* These are crazy thoughts. A computer can't have sex. The film was crap. He can barely remember it. Face it: Stanley has all the intelligence of washing machine. Stanley is just a machine programmed to do certain tasks in certain ways. His speaking parts are recordings. Stanley lacks consciousness. Stanley can't do original thinking. Stanley is as harmless as an electric toothbrush. Aaron is beginning to feel tired. Wants to lie down. But the floor is cold, apart from being rough and hard. He settles down as best he can but can't get comfortable. Lying on his back doesn't work. Lying on his side doesn't work. In the end he rests his buttocks on the floor and leans over, legs bent, to rest his head against his knees, his clasped hands held against his shins. He wonders what the time is. How long has he been in this dark room? Ten minutes? Twenty? This is all so bloody stupid. It's ridiculous. Irritably he gets to his feet. He sets off to the nearest wall. A long, straight trudge across a cold rough concrete floor. On and on and on. Meeting nothing. In the end he stops. This is beyond his understanding. It's as if he's somehow walked out of one room and into a vast underground chamber. But, oddly, the floor has the same consistency as that of the storage room. The same concrete; the same slightly serrated surface. But even an underground chamber has to have walls. And where's that filing cabinet? Where's the spade? With the spade he could force the door open – assuming it's jammed. He sighs. Get a grip, Aaron. Start walking and as you walk, count. One, two, three... twenty-eight, twenty-nine... eighty-three, eighty-four... one-hundred-and-fourteen... two-hundred-and-sixty-nine... five-hundred-and-ninety-one... seven-hundred-and-three... nine-hundred-and-ninety-nine, one thousand. This can't be real. Also he needs a piss. He takes hold of his old familiar friend. He hears the splatter. A splash falls on his right foot. Drops of warmth. He steps five paces to his left side and then continues walking. After what might be ten minutes he halts. Has another attempt to figure out what's happening. Since this cannot be real it must be imaginary. His perceptions have been warped. A chemical warping. A drug of some sort. *Acid.* That old mind-bending substance favoured by hippies back in California in the 1960s. Timothy-somebody was their guru. Tune in, drop out – something like that. LSD. Lysergic acid. Someone's slipped him some. Liquid. *That pouch of water on the flight.* The Dutch were notorious drug-users. Someone having a laugh? Like in *The Good Nurse*, except that instead of injecting insulin it's LSD. A distinct possibility. Aaron remembers that time KLM failed to load his case at Schiphol. It was delivered to Serena Lodge the next day. Oddly, white van man turned out to be a dwarf, who drove using an adapted seat and an extended steering wheel. The dwarf was jovial. He'd winked at Aaron. 'It's the wacky baccy,' he explained, gesturing at the case. Aaron understood him to mean that it was the penchant for cannabis smoking among Dutch baggage handlers that had delayed his suitcase. Then again, there was Becky's cappuccino. Does his P.A. hold a secret grudge? He can't think of any reason why she'd be hostile. He has always treated her well. As for the wine with dinner. He'd uncorked it himself. That could be ruled out. Aaron is quite certain that French wine producers don't tamper with their product – at least, not in that way. But whatever the source, the consequence is plain. He's on a weird trip. His body is probably sitting on the floor in the storage room, while his dream-body goes walkabout. He's probably squatting, giggling inanely in the dark, while his alter ego goes for a wander, trying to make sense of what on the face of it is inexplicable. Yes, that's it. He's in the storage room, paralysed by a drug. Prone. On the cold floor, helpless. His mind wandering. In a sort of dream. Or is it Esther? A stupid accident. His wife is into fads. She still reads *The Guardian*, for Christ's sake. The lifestyle section is her guide through that worrisome valley of darkness that is the unfashionable. If a *Guardian* harpy tells her to buy wooden clogs with yellow stripes, she buys wooden clogs with yellow stripes. Also foraging is still cool. *The Guardian* advises its shrunken readership holed-up in affluent urban London and a similar handful of well-heeled oases to wander out and collect driftwood for their log burners, whilst searching the woods for herbs and edible grasses. Esther is one of those rare readers who can actually make this action plan a reality. Aaron groans. He remembers she's a keen mushroom picker. His heart – what's left of that hard, withered organ – twists like the bleak self-mocking smile shaped by his lips. It plummets. There is a strange gravity here. And inside him that voice again. A commentator prone to sarcasm. A worm, wriggling. A whisperer, who whistles. Oy! With each proof correction your world changes a little. Oy! Aaron recalls that delicious lamb stew. He distinctly remembers it contained mushrooms. Esther had chattered about sourcing the ingredients locally but he hadn't really been paying attention. He understands now what she's done. She's inadvertently picked a magic mushroom. Its hallucinogenic properties have kicked in. His brain is frying. And all because his wife reads the fucking *Guardian*. Jesus... *Go*. Eh? He's just arrived at his conclusion about the mushroom when he hears a whispered half-word. *Goh*. A hard 'g' and the ghost of a sigh. It's not the worm voice (says the worm voice). Perhaps this is an auditory effect of that damned mushroom. It's as if someone had begun to speak, then changed their mind. Someone unseen, at the far end of this chamber. This chamber which is half real and half imaginary. He strains to listen but now there's nothing. He stands here, letting the minutes slide by. His pulse has begun another drum solo inside his head. He senses he's not alone in here. But he knows this isn't real. All the same, it's a little unnerving. His armpits release a sudden trickle of sweat. The tributaries snake down the sides of his rib cage. He feels thirsty. Has the beginnings of a headache. Panic rises in his chest. Aaron's face is hot and sticky. This whole situation is just too bloody absurd. It angers him. What a stupid bitch Esther is, picking wild mushrooms. It's not as if they can't afford to buy them. And it's not as if mushrooms aren't a cheap product. They're only bloody fungus. He feels ridiculously vulnerable, naked and lost in his own house. Him! An architect! How much some of his jealous competitors would enjoy seeing him now, like a child scared of that moment when mummy puts the bedroom light off. His bowels feel loose and restless. He's never going to leave that bed naked again. Next time he'll slip on his shorts and top and take his phone with him. He should never have put himself in this situation. Abruptly Aaron starts running. He holds out his arms, though he knows he won't collide with anything. He runs like someone fleeing from an atrocity where the shooter is still putting bullets into screaming civilians. His soft penis slaps wildly to and fro against his inside thighs. On and on he goes, minute after minute, until finally he halts, exhausted. He sits down, his rump resting on the rough, cold floor, and once again leans forward to rest his head on his bent knees. He begins to sob.

Later he raises his head, aware of a glimmer of light. He strains to see what it is. Some thirty metres away. An old-fashioned oil lamp. A metal contraption with an ornamental cap. A faint light spreading out from the bulbous glass. As his eyes adjust to the sight Aaron realises there's an old man standing just beyond the lamp. An ancient, wrinkled olive-skinned man. An Arab. He looks about seventy, which probably means he's ninety. Or fifty. Either way he just gazes back at Aaron, without emotion. That stare is discomforting. And then, mercifully, the old man starts to dissolve. A part of his head vanishes, along with his torso, an arm, a leg. It continues until at last there's just a fragment of his face left, a curl of parchment containing a single staring eye. And then that, too, goes. The oil lamp flickers and goes out. Aaron sighs. He guesses it's a trick but he needs to test it, just to be sure. He gets up and walks towards where the lamp rested on the concrete floor. He walks slowly, cautiously, not wanting to trip over the lamp when he gets to it. But of course it's not there. He must have walked sixty paces, seventy. One hundred. One-hundred-and-twenty. It's not there. Aaron sits down, his rump resting on the rough, cold floor, and once again leans forward to rest his head on his bent knees. He's alone in the darkness again. Time passes. It's a blur. Minutes, hours. Without his phone or a watch he's lost. Finally, shivering, he hears a cow, mooing. WTF? A *cow?* In here with him? Confirmation of his mushroom hypothesis. Indubitably. *Mooo...* Jesus. It's loud. It's near. But: *there's no way a cow could have got inside Serena Lodge.* It's just not possible. And then a beam of light shines from far above. A pure clean-cut beam. WTF? His brain is definitely frying. This cannot be happening, *tangibly.* It's surely only in his mind. A bright beam of light, making a circle on the concrete floor. About a metre in diameter. Theatrical. It makes him flinch, this sudden unexpected brightness. He screws up his eyes. It's like that time Jasmine dragged him to a Beckett play in Manchester. That had beams of light. People in pots, just their heads sticking out. When the light shone on them the cast talked. It was crap. Boring. No action at all. But *she* thought it was brilliant. Jasmine the actress. White face, scarlet lipstick, purplish eye makeup, straight black hair which fell to her shoulders.

Jasmine: tall and thin. Tiny breasts, not much bigger than golf balls. Her rib cage was oddly protuberant. It pressed into him as he lay on top of her. She dumped him after three fucks. Didn't realise he was married, she said. Was quite fierce about it, LOL. Had whoever was orchestrating this shit attended the same production? No, don't be silly. It's not orchestrated. It's simply his brain, still frying in its pan. But *so real.* It's surely the same lighting engineer at work as at the Royal Exchange. Hired by the billionaire behind this drama. It's like *The Magus.* He's being played. Except that his Conchis has yet to put in an appearance. Maybe it's Esther's father. He's set a detective on his trail to check up on his son-in-law. He doesn't like what the report says. Having found Aaron guilty he's now starting the punishment schedule. Sam Cohen. A dangerous man to displease. HellBite Systems had protection. There were rumours of links and connections to certain intelligence agencies. Aaron had chosen never to enquire into his father-in-law's business. But no, Sam had always been genial. He was proud his daughter had married a distinguished architect (apart from that other important consideration). No, can't be Sam who is responsible. He wouldn't choose theatre. Not this. The beam projecting down on to empty space. A circle of blazing light illuminating a patch of concrete floor about forty metres away. Aaron realises that means there's a rig up there. Perhaps a platform. Maybe there's a ladder fixed to the wall. If only he could find it... *Mooo...* That damn cow again. Behind him. As Aaron hears it the beam of light cuts out. He turns in the dark. *Mooo...* Did it jump over the moon to get here? Is the Cheshire cat going to put in appearance? Aaron manages to laugh. A low, bleak, thin laugh. The laughter echoes back at him, doubling, tripling, enlarging itself while it dies away. *Mooo...* A fresh beam of light comes out of the darkness above and fixes on the cow. It seems huge. It's a real cow, with a dangling dripping pink tongue, big stupid cow eyes and a dappled black and white coat. The eyes are Esther's eyes. That must be the magic mushroom. The cow placidly chews the grass rising from a rectangle of turf. The emerald colour of the grass makes it look artificial. Is it Astro Turf? Aaron walks towards the cow, which continues munching the unreal-looking grass. He notices there's a QR code on its cheek. If only he had his phone with him... Also, towards the animal's rear, is a large barcode. Black and white stripes and the number 9781838489830. He's about ten metres from the cow when it defecates. A liquid gush, pouring from its anus as though at the turning of a tap. A whiff of excrement drifting into his nostrils. Oddly, it's white shit, not brown. WTF? Aaron knows that sometimes, very rarely, dog shit is white. Loudon Wainright III sang about it. It's not something he chooses to remember. The sloppy torrent ceases, leaving a sloppy dome. The cow goes on chewing the emerald turf. And then it turns its head and faces him. 'Hello, Aaron.' Jesus. A talking cow! On its brow he sees the branded letters TM. WTF? This is *Alice-in-Wonderland* territory. *Totally*. 'I've been expecting you.' The cow is very nicely spoken, Aaron has to give it that. She's obviously been to a very good school. There is some comfort there. 'You have?' 'I need you.' 'You do?' 'Milk me.' WTF? 'I'm bursting. My teats cry out for your smooth, gentle hands.' It's true. The udder looks bloated. This cow definitely needs milking. 'But there's no bucket.' 'Look again, Aaron.' In the blink of an eye a stainless-steel bucket appears, clean and shiny as a milking bucket should be. 'Hey, what about a milking stool?' 'You have to be kidding. Just kneel, bitch.' Did he hear right? Did the cow really use that word? 'Did you just –' 'Don't speak until spoken to.' 'But –' 'If you want to get out of here, do what I say. Otherwise it's endless night for you, buddy.' Aaron falls silent. 'Kneel and start squeezing.' 'But I don't know how to do it.' The cow chuckles. 'I must be the first gal you ever said that to!' 'What's your name?' 'Elektra.' 'That's a lovely name.' 'Yes, it is, isn't it?' The cow farts, explosively. 'Actually, I lied. I'm known by another name. But in the interest of narrative suspense I'm withholding it at present.' 'Cool.' 'Enough idle chit-chat. Get on your knees, as the Archbishop said to the actress.' 'Okay.' Aaron kneels. 'Now what?' 'You see my four teats? Think of them as taps to four separate containers. Take hold of the front two first, one in each hand. Unless you are a superhero and can manage all four at once. But I don't think you're a superhero, are you, Aaron?' 'He does not reply. 'You basically take a firm grip around the base of the teat, then squeeze downward. Try it. I'm sure you'll soon get the hang of it.' The hard bare floor is painful to kneel on. But he feels warmer now. The cow seems to radiate heat. Close to, it seems enormous. He soon gets it right. But there's a shock. 'Your milk is blue!' The cow farts. 'Of course it is.' 'Why *of course*?' 'Just fill the bucket, buster. Remember what I said about endless night.' Aaron perseveres. Slowly he fills the bucket. He moves on from the first two teats to the last two. The emptied chambers of the udder go wrinkled. Aaron is reminded of a half-deflated inflatable bed. That thought makes him think of Sarah. Once he's finished the bucket looks like it's filled with blue paint. His knees ache. Aaron gets to his feet. He sways a little. The bright beam of light continues to pour down on him. It feels ridiculously theatrical. He half imagines an audience out there in the darkness, watching silently. 'May I speak?' The cow defecates sloppily again, then says: 'If you must.' 'I wanted to ask how you came to be inside my house.' 'That would be telling.' 'So what happens next?' 'That's easy. I tell you who I am and then I vanish. The light goes out and you find yourself alone in the dark again. But don't worry. There will be one or two dramatic developments before you reach the end.' 'The end of what?' The cow grins. 'That would be telling. Moooo! Moooo!' 'Are you being sarcastic?' 'Cows don't do sarcasm. Anyway, let's cut to the chase. I want you to step backwards ten paces. Then I'll tell you who I am.' 'Okay.' Aaron steps backwards. One, two, three, four, five, six, seven, eight, nine, ten. He stands there, expectant. The cow moves sideways, taking care not to kick the bucket. Now its rear end faces him. Aaron sees that two more letters are branded on the animal's rump, one each side of its anus. An H and a J. It reminds him he meant to ask Elektra-who-is-not-Elektra what the meaning of all these symbols is. 'Moooo!' The sound bounces off the distant walls and echoes, giving the impression of an entire herd of bellowing cattle. When it finally fades away the cow speaks. 'I am the Auschwitz cow,' it says in a sombre voice. 'I get milked twice a day.' Then the beam of light cuts out and Aaron is in the darkness once again. He stands there, startled, then quickly moves forward, hands outstretched. One, two, three, four, five, six, seven, eight, nine, ten... *Fuck!* His left shin collides with the milking bucket and a stab of acute pain shoots up his leg. That hurt. *That fucking hurt.* He hears the bucket tip and spill its contents, followed by the sound of it rolling away with a clatter on the cold floor. The Astro Turf doesn't seem to be there any more. 'Where are you, cow?' he shouts. Ow, ow, ow, ow, ow, ow, say the walls of this place. Aaron walks on. He continues at a steady pace for ten minutes. But he still doesn't come to any wall. A sudden nausea afflicts him. Before he can stop it his bowels boil, his sphincter opens, and a slush of diarrhoea pours down his inside thigh and splatters on the floor. A foul stench rises to his nostrils. He hurries on. He's been counting his steps but now he's lost the number. His head feels fuzzy. He's lost track of time. It's colder now but his brow feels feverish. He can feel the shit clinging to the skin of the insides of his legs. He goes on. And on. On until he drops. Sinks to the cold floor, exhausted. Lies on his stomach. Feeling very unwell. Feeling feverish. His stomach and his head both hurt. A steady throbbing. Arms stretched out, legs straight. His scrotum hurts too. Feeling very unwell. Feverish, yes. Throbbing. The smell makes him retch. His throat is dry. His throat burns. His stomach burns. He feels like puking but nothing will come. Shivers. Lies there for he does not know how long. No sense of time, now. And in the end closes his eyes, sleeps. Asleep. Asleep. How long? Doesn't know. Is disorientated, totally. And now the blackness is alive with white, drifting specks. Are his eyes open or closed? See! Up there! Andromeda, Cassiopeia. Unmistakeable. Aaron knows his constellations. And now the stars change, become thicker, whiter. May blossom whirls down a Hampshire lane. He drives into it. His mother has just died. The blossom hits his windscreen like snow, like a blizzard. White specks, dancing. The flow continues, becomes monotonous. That constellation up there, out of focus. Must be the Pleiades. He is eight years old. His father is showing him the night sky. They have a Charles Frank astronomical telescope. His father built it from a kit. Aaron goes indoors and brushes his teeth. He puts on his pyjamas and gets into his little bed. He reads a few more pages of *The Hitchhiker's Guide to the Galaxy*, then puts out the light. Sleeps. Sleeps until it ends. It ends as abruptly as it began. It ends with a sudden sharp fluttering sound. It wakes him. He lies there listening to it. Flutter-flutter. And then a deeper sound, a sort of clicking. A humming. It's the three fluorescent tubes coming back to life. A few flashes of light and then they all come on, flooding the room with illumination. He's back where he started. Where he came in. Groaning, he gets to his feet. He feels terrible. The stench is appalling. Looks around. He's in the storage room. The red filing cabinet still stands in the corner, unblemished. The silver-bladed spade nearby. Everything is exactly the same, except for the messes on the floor. A puddle of piss. Splatters of brown stinking mess. Footmarks, where he's trodden in shit. Long brown smears. Disgusting. Loathsome. As he stares at it the door swings open behind him. He turns and rushes towards it. Half expecting it to slam in his face and the lights to go out. Doesn't happen. He's out in the corridor, sobbing. Stares down at his filthy, encrusted legs. *Jesus.* Must have a shower, get clean. He makes his way back up to the floor where the guest bedrooms are. Goes into the first one and heads for the en-suite. Into the shower cubicle. A spray of hot water drenching him, soaking his hair, pouring down his torso, washing away the shit. The stench of it rising from the shower tray while it vanishes down the drain. Aaron slathers himself in lemon-scented body lotion. Gets himself clean. Soon all the shit's gone. He's himself again. Steps out of the cubicle and towels himself dry. He slips on the white towelling robe which hangs from the hook. That's better. He heads for the kitchen. Sees it's still only 3.12am. He's been in the storage room for a little under two hours. He finds the bottle of brandy and pours himself a slug. The fire runs through his veins. Already he feels so much better. But he's hungry. He finds the tin of Matzos crackers. Takes out three. Smears them with butter and adds some slices of crumbly Caerphilly. He picks out a bunch of green grapes from the bowl. He makes a black coffee and adds a spoonful of honey. Hot and sweet. He takes his feast out on to the guest level balcony. It's still a gorgeous night. Strangely warm, despite the hour. Moonlight illuminates the acres of marsh reed. The distant River Blyth is a thread of silver, winding among banks of mud that look electroplated. Silent night, Holy night... Aaron farts. He sits on a metal chair by one of the circular tables and wolfs down this midnight feast. He's feeling much better already. His fever has gone. Ditto the pain in his stomach and head. Ditto the throbbing. He still can't make sense of any of it, though. His best guess is the magic mushroom theory. Some kind of hallucination. But it's over, that's the main thing. He goes back to the kitchen, still ravenous. More crackers and cheese. Another coffee. Also a chocolate éclair from the pack in the fridge. Esther is hooked on them. It's a pregnancy thing. Replete, he stands by the railing. Needs a piss. Can't be arsed to go to one of the guest bedrooms. Aaron opens the towelling robe and slips his penis between the bars of the railing. Pisses down into the garden. A long, silent, satisfying jet. That's better. And now a new desire forms. All that stress, all that fucked-up weird storage room shit. He needs some relief. Goes back to the kitchen. Takes another chocolate éclair. He goes back to the balcony. He pushes the circular table up against the balcony, then slips off his towelling robe. He climbs up on to the table and kneels at the edge. He takes the chocolate éclair and opens it up, scooping out the cream. Aaron presses the cream against his penis. It's cold, strangely arousing. He begins to squeeze his longest love. The old up and down. He's erect very quickly. The cream drips through his fingers. He smears some of it on his taut scrotum. Deliciously cold. As he moves slowly towards his climax he suddenly sees her. Down there, right below him, on what used to be the old public footpath. There were two cutting across the land he needed. This was the one he *did* manage to get diverted. Now somewhat overgrown. It's a girl, mid-twenties maybe. Plump. Black boots, blue jeans, a check shirt. A blonde. She's standing there, framed by a pair of small conifers, looking directly up at him. The moonlight shines brightly on both of them. He sees that she's grinning. She gives a little wave, then moves her hand to her neck. She begins to unbutton her top. Slips it off, exposing a pair of large breasts. And now her hand is at her waist, unbuckling her leather belt. She unzips her jeans, and pulls them down, exposing a wondrous crop of wheat-coloured hair. She lets her jeans drop down to settle around her boots. Her right hand begins its work inside that glorious triangle. Oh yes, baby. Oh Jesus yes. Aaron's hand speeds up, he's getting there, he's almost there. Any minute now. *Oh shit!* To his horror his engorged penis pulls away from his crotch. His hand jerks upward and he finds himself holding his prick in front of his face. His crotch wells with black blood. *Oh Jesus.* Down below the girl instantly decomposes. He sees now she's just a scrap of pale plastic sheeting, entangled on thorns. Aaron gets off the table, penis in hand. Weirdly, it's still stiff, like a kitchen roll tube. But that gash under his pubic hair is squirting blood. *Jesus.* Aaron runs naked to the kitchen, leaving a trail of blood. He tears open the door of the freezer and drops his penis in the top drawer, between two containers of frozen milk. He scrabbles in one of the lower drawers and finds the ice-cubes. He takes the tray to the worktop and smashes it against the mock-marble surface. He scoops up the ejected cubes and takes them back to the freezer. He packs them around his penis (which seems smaller now). *Oh Jesus.* He grabs the kitchen towel and presses it against the bloody gash between his legs. Then he runs to the master bedroom. Weird. The door won't open. Surely she's not locked it. Aaron thumps on it. 'Esther! *Esther!* Let me in!' He keeps banging on it. What's the stupid bitch up to? Has she taken a pill? Finally she replies. 'No.' Her voice sounds cold, almost metallic. 'For fuck's sake, Esther! This is an emergency! I need my phone. I have to get to hospital! This is serious!' 'Tough.' 'Jesus, Esther! My dick just came off! I need to see a doctor!' 'A likely story. Do you think I'm an idiot? I'm not letting you in.' 'What are you playing at, darling? I'm not kidding. I need help! Urgently!' 'I'm not letting you in.' 'Why not, for fuck's sake?' 'Because we're through. I've had enough. I'm divorcing you.' *'What? Why?* Jesus, what's come over you, sweetybear?' 'I'm not your sweetybear. Not any longer. I'm going to be your ex-wife. Wife number two.' 'Don't do this to me, Esther! Let me in.' 'NO.' 'I'll bleed to death. I'll die!' 'GOOD.' 'Why are you doing this to me? For Christ's sake, Esther.' 'I KNOW WHAT YOU'VE BEEN UP TO.' 'What's that supposed to mean?' 'Your deceit. Your relentless philandering.' 'Honey, baby, I swear –' 'Don't lie to me, Aaron. I know all about what you got up to in Tel Aviv.' 'Baby, I swear –' 'With Renata. Remember her? I rather think you do. She told you you could do *anything* you wanted. And I know *exactly* what you did. It makes me sick. You're perverted. You aren't fit to be the father of my child. Of anyone's child.' 'Honestly darling, don't believe Renata. She's a liar! She's just out to make trouble. Don't let her come between us!' 'As for Amsterdam. How could you? With *a common whore*. It makes me sick just to think about it. I may have caught a disease.' 'Honestly, darling. I really –' 'Don't *honestly* me you devious prick.' 'Please. Let me in. I'm hurt. I'm hurt real bad.' 'More lies. I've had enough. I'm starting divorce proceedings. We're through. You can go and fuck that bitch at your office for all I care.' 'Esther, darling – *I have to get to a doctor.*' 'Fuck off. I'm not opening the door. That's final.' His fists batter the door. He sobs with rage and despair. 'I'll smash it down!' 'You designed it so it couldn't be broken down. Remember?' He did, yes. It's true. *Jesus.* But his phone and his car keys are in the bedroom. 'At least let me have my phone and car keys.' 'Fuck off.' '*Please!*' 'And another thing. This baby I'm having. It's not yours. It's George's. Remember him? The gardener. I've been shagging him for over a year. Ever since I found out about you and that girl in Cromer.' Aaron feels his bowels churn. He feels sick. 'There is no girl in Cromer!' 'You're pathetic, Aaron. I've met Sally. So young, so naïve. But very attractive, I agree. She told me she had no idea you were married. You know what, Aaron? I might be more sympathetic if you had a shred of honesty. But you've lost all sense of what truth is. It must be awful to be you.' It's hopeless. And he's losing blood. He runs back to the kitchen. He searches the cupboards until he finds where she keeps the Tupperware. He grabs a penis-sized box and takes it to the freezer, wrenches open the top drawer. Oh God. Oh Jesus. Oh fuck. His prick has shrunk. It's not much bigger than a cocktail sausage. And it looks deathly white. Aaron puts it in the box and crams the ice-cubes on top of it. Then he runs back to the balcony, puts the towelling robe on, and goes quickly downstairs. He'll head for the road. Sooner or later there's bound to be someone driving in or out of Walberswick. He'll get them to phone 999 then drive him up the A12 to Lowestoft. They can meet the ambulance half way. He makes it down to the front door. He doesn't have a key to get back in but what the hell. He shuts it and runs towards the tunnel. Four minutes later he reaches the final gate. He scrambles over it, clutching his precious plastic box. But the front of his towelling robe is now stained by blood. It takes on a fan shape as it spreads out. The blood just won't stop pouring from his crotch. He feels strangely weak. Here, on the far side of the gate, he collapses. Loses consciousness. When he wakes he sees that clouds have rolled overhead, shutting out the stars. The moon has gone and the canopy of trees is no longer visible. Aaron shivers. The ground feels hard. His fingers touch a faintly serrated surface. The stink of faeces washes over him. He feels his right leg and touches dried shit. The white towelling robe isn't on him. He's lost his precious box. He reaches for his crotch. His prick is still there. Shrivelled, limp, but tangible. An awful realisation hits him. It can't be, no, please. It's not possible. He gets to his feet. Absolute blackness. There's nothing to be seen. No shapes, no shadows. *Nothing*. He screams a harsh loud scream and hears it reach a distant wall and return, echoing. There can't be any doubt. This is a cheap trick. The oldest trick in the book. He's back in the storage room. *He never left it*. He groans and gets to his feet. He sets off again. He keeps going. He's counting his steps now. Fifty-seven. Six-hundred-and-twenty. One-thousand nine-hundred-and-eighty-three. Two-thousand-and-fifty-six. Two-thousand-and-fifty-nine. He must surely have walked a mile by now. He keeps going until the blisters rise on his feet. Four miles, he reckons. It's insane; impossible. He lies down again, to the old discomfort. The fever has returned. A voice – a brisk, British upper-class voice – says 'You don't belong here.' Or did he imagine it? It wasn't worm. Or perhaps it was worm doing an impersonation. Mimicry. Tom Ripley up to his tricks again. He sleeps. He wakes. How long has he been here? He feels hungry. His bladder aches. He gets to his feet and stands and pisses into the darkness. A few splashes land on his toes but he doesn't care any more. He has a raging thirst. A desperate desire for a cold pint of Czech lager. A glass of milk or water. Anything, any liquid at all. He walks on. His feet are blistered, now. But two of the blisters on his feet have burst and it's agony to walk. Now he can only limp. He manages another half mile and then suddenly steps into something soft and slippery. Disgusted, he realises he's trodden in his own shit. Again, again. He's past caring. He limps on. Later he lies down again and sleeps. 'Aaron, darling, are you there?' It's Esther, calling to him. She sounds some distance away. At the end of the corridor perhaps. He opens his mouth to reply but his voice has gone. All that emerges from between his lips is a feeble, arid whisper. She goes on calling but it's obvious she can't hear him and finally she stops. The thirst is the worst. *Ha ha that rhymed!* The worst thing of all, the last words. Words all that's left. The last word that's left. *Verisimilitude.* A glorious word. A gorgeous word. It shines like oil in a puddle. Rainbow-hued. It slips through you like a fiery throbbing warming malt. Feverish. He's woken by an explosion. The ground shakes. A flash of light shows an advancing wall of smothering white dust. Even as he sees it the cloud rushes at him, making him choke. Dust gets in his mouth and up his nose. He starts coughing. Aaron sways in the darkness. Commas hook on to his tongue. Full stops dance across his closed lids, burning. Colons are a whore's eyes, beside him on the bed. A semi-colon is an obscene thing. An exclamation mark is a fallen prick that emits a solitary grey drop. Water water, everywhere! He hears its roar. It's slapping against the flanks of the house. The river is in flood. It's cracking the walls. Drops are starting to fall, tapping on the floor like a wireless operator on a sinking liner, urgently requesting assistance. Water! Aaron crawls slowly towards the delicious sound. He crawls on and on and on. He crawls on, never reaching those enticing drips. He knows what the problem is. It's time to set things straight. A terrible mistake has been made. 'I'm Jewish!' he sobs and the sound of this last word repeats and bends and flows on inside him. Wish wash ash washer fash wish fasher basher fash cash fash lash fash lasher masher fasher mush fash slush, *shhhh, shhhh, shhhh.* Now he can't even crawl. Aaron lies on his back, staring up. This, Aaron realises, is the end. Not only is he going to die, he isn't even going to have the satisfaction of an explanation. *How? Who? Why?* A question mark is like a drop of blood falling from a meat hook. Mush fasher slush. A limp prick. Prick there? Gone? The horror. Can't feel it. Feel what? Drips, wet. Filth slush. Between the sh... Shush now. Shit flow. Flow continues until. Until finally stops. Word flow ends also. Tonic gone flat. A twist of lemon. Along with... Along with a failing congested. Leathery old. Pump. His perishable. Huh? Ha, ha... Huh. Heart-hurt. Or is this? Also? Missing? Gone.

SUDOXE

1

It begins with the black outline of three raised cut-out arms set against a plain deep blue background. The arm which reaches the highest holds the stock of a weapon, probably a rifle, which is snapped-off cleanly beyond the part containing the trigger and the bolt. Below this stark image a single flame burns, releasing black smoke. But it begins earlier than that with the words *The airplane plip-plopped down the runway to a halt before the big sign: WELCOME TO CYPRUS*. And it begins before that, at The Red House on Yarkon Street. And it begins before that, at 4 Carlton Gardens, London, on a Friday in July, over a century ago. And it begins before that, too. So many beginnings, with only one ending. But that ending is not yet ended.

2

It's a movie, a bestseller, and the second book of that collection of myths, fictional stories and theological propaganda known as The Old Testament. *Exodus*. Or as Ellis prefers to call it: *Zudoxe*. Because the novel and the movie reverse history. They tip the truth on its head. They twist, pervert, fantasize. And they preface that stew with the slashing, violent Z of Zionism. No coincidence that the same jagged consonant is found in Zionism's twin blood-and-soil ideology...

3

It's time to reverse that reversal, Ellis thought. It was hot and he was bored and there was a global pandemic. On this day he was as hot as the main character in *The Day the Earth Caught Fire*. Nothing bored Ellis more than contemporary literary fiction.

Earlier that year *The Times* had reproduced the text of a seminal Sally Rooney story. *Marianne and Connell, the stars of Sally Rooney's novel* Normal People, *now the hit TV series, first appeared in* At the Clinic, *a short story published in* The White Review. *We reprint it here.* Ellis had looked at the text. *So you know, I broke up with Lauren. I don't know if you heard that. For a moment she pretends to be engaged in reading. He can see she's deciding what to do or say. The workings of Marianne's mind become transparent to him in brief flashes like this before they recede again.* The story is about two twenty-three-year-olds who have intermittent sex. It's about their feelings, their thoughts. The prose is flat, uninteresting. It describes what Marianne feels about Connell and what Connell feels about Marianne. It's lifestyle fiction. Ellis felt a deep alienation from so much of the politics and the culture which surrounded him. And a great fatigue. That fatigue extended to his own writing, where he permitted the occasional reflexive pronoun. He did not always see eye to eye with his editor, whose commitment to grammar was sharper than Sharp's. But more than that, what was there to write about that was worth writing about? Another day and your mood changes. Now, quite suddenly and unexpectedly, on Saturday 8th August 2020, he had a basis for a new short text. He remembered Marx. Confronted by Proudhon's *The Philosophy of Poverty* he'd produced a sardonic reversal: *The Poverty of Philosophy*. In that first year of the global pandemic Ellis had done a lot of reading, mainly non-fiction. He'd watched various movies and spent many hours on the internet. Now he began with *Zudoxe* the movie. The novel and the Bible could wait. He watched it through, then started watching it again, more slowly this time, freeze-framing the images, jotting down notes. The opening credits were by Saul Bass. A Hollywood legend. A design pioneer. A Jew. Ellis knew his work from *Psycho* and *North-by-Northwest*. Three raised arms and a rifle – a symbol of struggle involving weaponry – militant Zionism – set against a plain deep blue background. That deep blue. The Mediterranean? The Israeli flag? The boundless blue sky? This is a movie where it never rains and where there's never a cloudy day. And that flame. The fire of nationalism? The solitary flame of remembrance? Ellis remembered as a child being taken to the Arc de Triomphe and seeing the eternal flame. In the Saul Bass credits sequence the flickering flame from which an oily black smoke rises seemed more like an allusion to the Nazi genocide, Ellis felt. At the end the tongue of flame turns into a wall of fire. Surely this invokes the incineration of Jewish corpses in the ovens of the death camps? *Zudoxe* the movie constantly invokes the Nazi genocide. It begins with survivors arriving to be interned in camps by British troops. That word *camps* resonates. The Jews escape to the freedom of Palestine. There they only want to co-exist with the Arabs. But the Arabs are in league with the Nazis and the only pro-Jewish Arab in the movie is murdered, with a swastika painted on the wall by the corpse. This is the risible and defamatory message of *Zudoxe*. Jews just wanted to live alongside the Palestinians but the Palestinians desired only to exterminate them or to depart and leave them, the Jews, to renew the barren and neglected land. *Zudoxe* reverses the historical truth in so many ways. It suddenly occurred to Ellis that there was one movie above all which ought to be compared to *Zudoxe*. That was Gillo Pontecorvo's *The Battle of Algiers*, released in 1966. Ellis ordered a DVD copy from Amazon. Then he moved on until he found a site on the internet where Saul Bass explained some of the meaning of his *Zudoxe* credit sequence. *The film is about Israel. In its earlier restricted form, the flame has the symbolic connotation of the Temple and the 'eternal light'. At the end of the title it provides a symbolic forerunner of the struggle for independence which is the main content of the film.* Ellis learned that the symbol and the flames were central features of the advertising campaign to promote the movie. Even the invitations to the premiere were deliberately scorched, to make them seem like historical documents. Joseph Goebbels would have been immensely impressed by this marketing, Ellis thought. He wasn't convinced by Bass's explanation. The word *holocaust* can mean a Jewish sacrificial offering burnt to ashes on an altar and it can also mean large scale destruction or death as a result of fire or war. Whatever else that fire in the credits sequence is meant to invoke, surely the destruction of European Jews is the primary one.

Besides, historically, the Nazi genocide was the first alibi of the Zionist state, just as today holocaust remembrance has been hijacked by Zionists for their own grotesque and repellent purposes.

4

Zudoxe had been shown (where else?) on BBC television years ago, and at the time Ellis had videotaped it. Then, when videotape began to be edged out, he transferred the movie to a pair of blank DVD disks. This meant that when he watched the movie it was prefaced by the BBC's anonymous voiceover introduction, describing it as: *Otto Preminger's story of the events that led to the birth of the state of Israel.* Which was a travesty. A true account of those events would have to begin with the origins of Zionism, the racist colonial fantasies of Theodore Herzl, the cultivation of British imperialism by Chaim Weizmann, Palestinian resistance to the colonisation of their country, the vicious repression by the British army of the Palestinian revolt in the years 1936-1939, and the cynical handover of Palestine to violent racist Jews by the superpowers – Truman, Stalin, the Attlee government. Almost every aspect of *Zudoxe* was a lie. The original *Exodus* saga was a Zionist publicity stunt. The ship never reached Palestine. *Zudoxe* tips reality on its head. Jewish terrorism and violence is never shown, apart from a glancing acknowledgement of the bombing of the King David Hotel. That terrorist act is sanitised by showing it only from a distance as a bang and a remote surge of smoke. The viewer's attention is instantly diverted by the hysterics of the blonde cutie Karen who has just emerged from a reunion with her long lost father, now in a vegetative state resulting from his concentration camp suffering. Cut to the daring escape of impetuous but sexy young Jewish Irgun bomber Dov Landau, who twice outwits the pursuing British troops. Apart from the one good Arab – played by a white American actor, naturally – the Palestinians have no existence, except as killers in league with Nazis. Palestinians are introduced early on in the movie as maniacs and brutal murderers of children.

The Jewish settlement in the movie has a statue in memory of a teenage Jewish girl. The Palestinians cut off her hands and her feet and they gouged out her eyes. That's the local Arabs for you. Pitiless torturers. The film climaxes with the burial of blonde cutie Karen, murdered by an anonymous white-robed Palestinian, alongside the good Arab, also murdered. A pious graveside speech by Paul Newman looks forward to peaceful co-existence with the Arabs. Then everyone jumps aboard a line of trucks and goes off to fight the Arabs. A stirring ending, set in the autumn of 1947. Ethnic cleansing made sexy and upbeat.

5

John Derek, actor, who played the good Arab in *Zudoxe*, said: *I never liked acting. Or my films*. Another time he said*: I'm not an actor but I'll turn up on time and know my words*. And, unusually for an actor, he was telling the truth. He quit. He preferred photography and directing. And, it would seem, sex. His first wife was Pati Behrs Eristoff, a grandniece of Leo Tolstoy. She was the only one of his four wives he did not photograph naked for *Playboy*. The lives of actors and actresses are sometimes – often? – far more interesting and dramatic than the characters they have played. Valerie Jill Haworth, who plays the blonde cutie, for example. She was born in Hove, Sussex. A town and county Ellis had once had some familiarity with. She died aged 65 and is buried in Valhalla. She'd been considered for the role of Lolita in the Kubrick adaptation. Spell-check declined to recognise this director's name. It suggested Ellis might like to consider Rubric, Cubic, Cupric or perhaps Kuris. In her first major movie appearance, in *Zudoxe*, Valerie Jill Haworth, who was then fifteen, plays fifteen-year-old Karen. Karen the blonde cutie falls in love with the sexy Irgun terrorist played by the actor Sal Mineo. But they do not have sex and the same night that Karen reveals her love for Sal Mineo's character she is murdered. But at some point after making the movie Valerie Jill Haworth and Sal Mineo started a relationship. They became engaged. Then Haworth broke off the relationship when she caught Sal having sex with a man. But they remained close friends. Looking at the list of movies the actor had starred in Ellis realised he'd seen Sal Mineo in *The Longest Day*. But he had no memory of which part he'd played.

6

For its racist stereotyping and propaganda content *Zudoxe* should really be filed alongside *The Birth of a Nation* and *Gone with the Wind*, Ellis thought.

7

Googling *exodus* Ellis kept coming across *Mad Men*. His spell-check software was plainly obsolete. It declined to recognise the verb *To Google*. It drew a disapproving wavy red line under *Googling*, like a school teacher. It suggested Ellis might be after Goggling, Goodling, Go ogling, Gouging or Gosling. Ellis smiled at *Go ogling*. He checked out the relevant episode of *Mad Men*. First season, episode six: *Babylon*. The year is 1960. The agency is offered an account to promote tourism in Israel. Don is seen reading the hardback edition of *Zudoxe*. He is trying to find an angle to sell vacations there. But it's a struggle. Not even his Jewish interest can help. As a storyline it doesn't seem to go anywhere. Don remarks that *Zudoxe* has less action than he was expecting. True. The first two hundred pages are surprisingly unpacy, with vast quantities of information dumping. And that 'information' is frequently false.

8

It's still 2020 in this early draft. On the *Electronic Intifada* website Ellis read: *A Palestinian child imprisoned by Israel has tested positive for the virus that causes COVID-19, amid an outbreak in Israeli detention centres. Israel arrested the 15-year-old from his home in the Jalazone refugee camp, near the occupied West Bank city of Ramallah, on 23 July. This is the first known case of a Palestinian child detainee contracting the virus.*

His identity is being protected by human rights group Defense for Children International Palestine for privacy reasons. Israeli forces transferred the child to the Shikma interrogation center in Ashkelon, southern Israel. They postponed his interrogation after he tested positive for the virus. But despite being infected, Israeli authorities extended the boy's detention for another eight days "since he has yet to be interrogated", according to the human rights group. Israel is currently holding the child at a police station in Acre in northern Israel. Which was interesting because this child is fifteen – the same age as Karen in *Zudoxe* – and Acre is where sexy Paul Newman helps to free his uncle and scores of other jailed Jews.

9

After the wall of fire the movie begins. The camera pans across a sunlit Cypriot panorama of mountains and open countryside. A solitary black car stands parked on a rough track below. A disembodied voice narrates the history of Cyprus as a land with many conquerors. The camera reaches the man who is telling this history. He is a brown-skinned guide and taxi driver. Listening to him is an elegantly-dressed blonde woman, Kitty Fremont, played by Eve Marie Saint, aged thirty-five. The man flatters her, telling her how much the British are admired on Cyprus. I'm an American, she dryly retorts. The man tells her how much Americans are liked on Cyprus. It is established that this olive-skinned man is a deceitful flatterer.

10

Another long hot day. 13 August 2020. **SUMMER MUST-READS: RECOMMENDATIONS FROM LITERARY AGENTS.** Anna David, Curtis Brown Creative, wrote: *I am excited to be taking Emily St John Mandel's new novel* The Glass Hotel. *I was blown away by her last novel* Station Eleven. Cathryn Summerhayes, Curtis Brown, wrote: *Chris Whitaker's* We Begin at the End *is a jaw-droppingly good novel that makes* *your heart race whilst breaking it at the same time. And for the nonfiction nature buff,* Diary of a Young Naturalist *by an immensely talented teenager will make you look at the world outside your window in a totally fresh way.* Stephanie Thwaites, Curtis Brown, wrote: *I absolutely loved and devoured the astonishing* True Story *by Kate Reed Petty, which was utterly gripping, brilliantly written, smart and bold and so unlike anything I've read before.* Ellis wondered why no one had ever written a feature in the corporate media about the corrosive influence of literary agents on contemporary literature. Or about lazy corporate publishers who allowed this pernicious adjective-sodden species to do all the thinking for them.

11

Roaming the internet Ellis came across an opinion piece posted by Greg Zimmerman on March 1st 2012, entitled *Does Anyone Still Read Leon Uris or James Michener?* Zimmerman was perturbed by the amount of Uris and Michener titles he came across in second-hand bookstores. Michener had died in 1997 and Uris in 2003. Zimmerman was worried these authors were *dying slow, torturous second deaths.* Although much of their work was still in print *these novels seem to be sliding slowly off the radar of most readers.* Zimmerman wrote: *This is impossibly sad. I don't think it's overstating things to say that these were world-changing writers.* He believed there were several historical novelists who continued in the great tradition of Leon Uris and James Michener – Bernard Cornwell, Edward Rutherford, Herman Wouk, John Jakes, Jeff Shaara, Colleen McCullough, Hilary Mantel – but alas, *they just don't hold the same allure for me as Michener and Uris.* But then, thought Ellis, who nowadays reads Marie Corelli or Edgar Wallace?

12

The Bible could not wait. Ellis began reading *The Second Book of Moses, Commonly Called Exodus.* He also started watching

Ridley Scott's *Exodus: Gods and Kings*. You could tell it was a movie without merit by the two review quotations on the DVD packaging. *A spectacular blockbuster*, said that well-known cinema publication the *Daily Star*. An observation which was, in any case, descriptive rather than analytical. *Epic cinema*, agreed that other critical journal, the *Sunday Mirror*. Ellis watched the movie over two days. It was an unsatisfactory production. The CGI was too obvious, giving the whole film a curious synthetic and unrealistic quality. The Egyptian scenes were soaked in a strange coppery light, as if filmed through a colour filter. Plus there were too many characters. Most of the characters had opaque names which Ellis struggled to decipher. The Egyptians were as hard to distinguish as the Hebrews (apart from Ben Kingsley and a couple of the women). There were faces which seemed vaguely familiar from other films or perhaps TV drama. Ellis noticed that the word *Jew* was carefully avoided. The opening sequence of on-screen explanation intimated, astonishingly, that the Jews had built the pyramids. As the film progressed Christian Bale began to resemble Charlton Heston. The only aspect of the movie that was at all original or interesting was its representation of the LORD as a small English boy who might well have wandered over from the set of *Lord of the Flies*.

13

As for odious Uris and *Zudoxe*. He reversed the truth, repeatedly. His information dumping was riddled with blatant misrepresent-ations. The British forced two thousand refugees on to the *Patgria* for exile to Mauritius, he claimed. 'The *Patria* sank off Palestine's shores in sight of Haifa, and hundreds of refugees drowned.' Uris makes it sound as if the ship sank through negligence. He omits to mention it was sunk by the Haganah, who blew it up. This act of terrorism was authorised by Moshe Sharett, later Prime Minister of Israel. Some two-hundred and sixty-seven passengers drowned and one-hundred and seventy-two were injured. Jews had killed Jews. As a damage limitation exercise the Jewish Agency then claimed that those on board had *deliberately* blown themselves up. It was Masada all over again! Pinhas Lavon, future Minister of Defence, was not happy with this fabrication but grudgingly agreed that there was no necessary link 'between the legend and the truth'. The Zionist rapist Arthur Koestler recycled the lie nine years later in his book *Promise and Fulfilment*. Nine years after the lying Arthur Koestler the lying Leon Uris in *Zudoxe* omitted the blowing-up altogether and made the British responsible for the deaths. And according to the blurb, Uris's trashy book has sold one million copies. A million readers have absorbed the numerous lies and systematic misrepresentations of a cynical Jewish racist.

14

The Jewish film director Otto Preminger had a brother, Ingo, who also worked in the movies. He was an agent. He was involved in cutting a deal in 1955 in which MGM commissioned Jewish wartime adventure-story writer Leon Uris to write a novel about the birth of Israel. Uris was a hot property after his war books *Battle Cry* and *The Angry Hills* had been bestsellers and been adapted into popular movies. MGM financed Uris's research in Israel and acquired the movie rights. Uris spent three years researching and writing the book. Otto Preminger said he saw the massive manuscript piled in boxes at his brother's house. *I started reading it after dinner and couldn't put it down. I sat up most of the night and when I finished I knew I wanted to make that film.*

15

Uris's novel is set in Palestine over a two-year period from late 1946 to late 1948. It features three broad conflicts: the British occupying forces versus the Jews; the Jews versus the Palestinians; the supposedly 'moderate' Haganah versus the hard-line Maccabees (a thinly-disguised Irgun). These conflicts are replicated by the rocky romances which develop between the American heroine Kitty Fremont and Haganah hero Ari Ben

Canaan and between teenage Karen and young Irgun tough guy Dov Landau, and the family tension between Ari's 'moderate' father Barak of the Jewish Agency and his Irgun uncle, Akiva. Upon publication in September 1958 the book became an immediate bestseller. It is still in print today.

16

Jon Kimche praised Uris's potboiler for its propaganda value. 'Uris put sex, success and "James Bondism" into Zionism,' he wrote (*Jewish Observer*, 27 April 1962). 'This is the image of Israel that is fixed now more firmly in the mind of the generations of today than is that projected by either Herzl, Weizmann and even Ben-Gurion,' he concluded, delighted. Jon Kimche. A Swiss Jew and a friend of George Orwell's in London. An ardent Zionist. When Kimche was nineteen he acquired a brother, David. Born in England, David Kimche used his sectarian ethnic privileges as a Jew to emigrate to Israel, where he eventually became Deputy Director of Mossad. All these European Jews, none of whom had the slightest connection with the Middle East, devoting their lives to violent colonialism, repression and propaganda.

17

In 1950 Otto Preminger had wanted to make a movie about the birth of Israel. It was to be titled *A Candle for Ruth*. Preminger considered John Garfield, then Kirk Douglas, for the lead role of an American who joins the fight for the Jewish state. But the project initially fell through. By 1958 MGM had lost interest in adapting Uris's novel. They felt it would annoy British viewers. It would surely also be banned in Arab states. Preminger snapped up the screen rights to *Zudoxe* for $75,000. United Artists agreed to finance the movie, to the tune of $3,006,000. The rights fee included a preliminary sum for Uris's services as screenwriter. But Preminger didn't like the screenplay which Uris came up with. *I don't think he can write dialogue*, the director complained. Also: *In telling a story he becomes too much of a partisan.* The relationship became prickly. In the end Preminger fired Uris. When the movie came out Uris denounced it as false to his book. Next Preminger used Albert Maltz. During November and December 1959 he worked on a script. But Preminger didn't like what Maltz had written. It was, he said, *too serious*. Preminger phoned Dalton Trumbo on December 10th. Trumbo, who had recently finished his work on *Spartacus*, agreed to take over.

18

Who was behind this new Zionist propaganda movie? Dore Schary ran MGM when the original commission was given to Leon Uris. Otto Preminger was a driving force in getting the movie made. *He was not a religious Jew per se*, his wife said. *But he was a political Jew*. Ah, yes. Just like the major Zionist fanatics – Weizmann, Ben-Gurion. They didn't give a toss about the Bible. But it was a valuable ideological tool in expelling the Palestinians from their land. The third figure who was instrumental in creating *Zudoxe* the movie was Max E. Youngstein, vice president of United Artists. With the financing sorted, Otto Preminger headed to Israel. It was July 1959. There he met up with his old friend Meyer Weisgal, whom he'd known thirty years earlier in Vienna. Weisgal was now in charge of the Weizmann Institute of Science in Rehovot. Weisgal introduced him to David Ben-Gurion and others who would smooth the way for the film's production. In November he went back to look for suitable locations. Meanwhile there was the question of casting. Eve Marie Saint was selected for the role of Kitty. *I had some ideas*, she said. But Preminger didn't use any of them. Actresses! For the hero, Ari Ben Canaan, Preminger chose handsome blue-eyed Paul Newman. Newman later tried to wriggle out of the role. He didn't like the movie. He thought it was *too cold and expository*. The most difficult role to cast was Karen. After auditioning hundreds of candidates, Preminger selected Valerie Jill Haworth, then fourteen.

19

On DVD extras the actors always gush about how the director is the best, most brilliant director they've ever worked with. And so easy to get along with! Scriptwriters are no different. Dalton Trumbo gushed to a reporter how marvellous it was working with Preminger. *I'm verbose and sentimental*, he simpered. *He has a sharpshooter's eye for verbosity and he knows how to assassinate sentimentality. He's also most helpful in construction. I had more pleasure working with Otto than with anyone in my life. More fun, more amusement, more tact, and, of course, more hard work.* It's strangely apt that Trumbo's first scene in *Zudoxe* features a shameless flatterer. Preminger joked to Trumbo that if *Zudoxe* turned out to be a failure he would blame Trumbo's script. Yeah, some joke...

20

Trumbo. An odd name. Trumpets, rum, Rambo came to mind. Spell-check declined to accept that Trumbo could be what Ellis meant to type. It suggested Turbo, Trump, Trombone, Rumba and Thumb. But what Trumbo mainly reminded Ellis of was Dumbo.

21

Paul Newman told a reporter that Preminger had *the reputation of being such a fascist asshole and he IS, on the set*. But then perhaps he remembered that this is not the sort of thing you should really confide to a reporter. *I found him articulate, informed, funny, absolutely loveable*, Newman gushed. Yeah, right...

22

In his critical biography of Preminger, Chris Fujiwara praises Trumbo for perceiving and solving a structural problem in the Uris novel. The novel fragments the historical story into three parts, Fujiwara asserts. There's the narrative of the ship, the narrative of the Haganah's rivalry with the Irgun, and the narrative of the conflict between the Zionists and the Palestinians (or as Fujiwara would have it, the Jews and the Arabs). Trumbo's solution, writes Fujiwara, was to emphasize throughout the film the impending UN vote on partition as the central factor in all the characters' motivation. He also wrote a note on the historical aspect. *By their willingness to compromise and to accept partition, the Jews persuaded the world of their reasonableness as opposed to the unreasonableness of Arab claims. This is regardless of the fact that actually the Jews, too, wanted the whole land for themselves. I choose to dramatize their perhaps reluctant acceptance of partition as a* **desire** *for it. It is better dramatically, and better for Israel that it be that way, rather than to dramatize their desire for* **all** *of it (which would place them on the level of the Arabs in the audience's mind). We have, by increasing the Arab menace (as we had) over the first script, run the risk of being a little unjust historically. We have covered the essence and the excuse for this injustice in Akiva's speech on injustice and justice for the Jews and Arabs. But I think it essential for our dramatic balance, for historical accuracy, and for audience believability, to hit it once again.* So now Ari says of the Arabs of Abu Yesha, 'This is their home as well as ours.' But that's not balance. Palestine never was the home of European Zionist immigrants. Their claim on the land was fraudulent. It was a fairy story. Nor were and nor are Jews a people in a national sense. That's another mendacious Zionist fantasy. Preminger softened the tone and content of Uris's rabid potboiler but just because he turns Taha into a sympathetic Arab and has Akiva and Sutherland briefly acknowledge that there might be an Arab case, that case is never made. As Fujiwara notes, Preminger's movie is one with an 'overarching commitment to the Zionist cause'. It can 'be criticized for suppressing the voices of Arabs in order to project Zionist myth.' In this movie the Jews beg the Arabs to stay and Ari discovers that the village of Abu Yesha is deserted. Its population has departed voluntarily. There is no Jewish terror, no expulsions. Historically, the movie is a travesty.

As was the novel. In his classic critique *On Zionist Literature* (1967), Ghassan Kanafani noted that 'one witnesses farcical battles that even Mickey Mouse would not dare replicate'. Translation by Mahmoud Najib.

With Dalton Trumbo's script now completed and ready to film, Preminger set out a shooting schedule lasting fourteen weeks. The crew assembled in Zionist-occupied Haifa in March 1960 and shooting began on the 27th in Paris Square. Paul Newman's relationship with Preminger was cold and critical. He suggested changes to the script where his character was concerned. Preminger wasn't interested. Newman found Ari too one-dimensional. He didn't like what he called 'the "superman" quality attributed to Ari Ben Canaan in the book and the film script.' Newman found the production 'chilly'. Leon Uris had modelled Ari on Moshe Dayan, Yigal Allon and Ygael Yadin, among others. Newman wanted to meet them in order to understand better his character. He wanted to see how they thought, their behavioural mannerisms. Preminger stopped that. *I'm the director and I'll tell you what to do*, he told Newman. John Derek was also prevented from meeting Arabs. Paul Newman offered some modifications to Ari's long final speech. Preminger bluntly rejected them. *If you want to compare which of us is more intelligent, I'll save you the trouble.*

On the day that shooting started an advert for the movie designed by Saul Bass appeared in American newspapers and on billboards in New York, Chicago and Los Angeles, where it was scheduled to open in December. Three advertising campaigns later in the year promoted the start of shooting in Jerusalem, in Cyprus, and the final day. The campaigns were a dazzling success. Advance ticket sales were in excess of a million bucks, a record.

Jean Wagner of *Présence du cinema* arrived in Galilee to observe the shoot. He found Preminger tyrannical to both his crew and his cast. *On the set he crushes them, abuses them, and poor Paul Newman must have often needed to call on all his patience to keep from exploding. He spends his time, next, winning them over again, which is easy for him, since his charm is as great as his culture. On the whole, in spite of everything, it's difficult to say that Preminger is loved.* But as a control freak, in total control, he was impressive: *The knowledge he had of this immense machine, in its least details, was stupefying.* Paul Kohn offered a softer version: *At lunch on the set, he takes his turn in a long queue together with drivers, technicians and extras. He will also personally go over to an extra, and congratulate him on work well done. He is extremely generous, unpredictable and accessible to all.*

27

Preminger was unhappy with the performance of a group of child actors on the set. He screamed *Cry, you little monsters!*

28

May 23rd, 1960. A crowd of extras assembles in the Russian Compound in Jerusalem for the UN partition announcement scene. It was on this day that David Ben-Gurion announced that Adolf Eichmann had been captured and brought to Israel. It took many takes – over fifteen, by one account – to co-ordinate the speech made from a balcony by the actor Lee J. Cobb playing Barak Ben Canaan and the crowd below. Meyer Weisgal was the lookalike actor playing David Ben-Gurion. The scene was eventually finished but in the end it was an assemblage of short takes and not the continuous shot Preminger had wanted. Lee J. Cobb never worked with Preminger again. The next month the company left Israel and moved to Cyprus. The movie was finished on July 3rd, on schedule.

29

The movie opened in New York on December 15th, 1960. Reviewers praised the performances but thought that at 212 minutes it was too long-winded. During a preview at which the director was present the comedian Mort Sahl stood up, turned to Preminger and quipped: *Otto, let my people go.*

30

The movie made $8 million during its initial release. It was a commercial success.

31

The movie, remarks Chris Fujiwara, is made up of speeches. *Characters explain to each other the interests, policies, and goals of the groups they represent, sometimes to persuade, sometimes to enlighten, and sometimes merely to state positions.* The film ends with, by movie standards, a lengthy funeral oration.

32

On the night of 12 February 1976 Sal Mineo was murdered in an alleyway outside his apartment home on 8567 Holloway Drive, West Hollywood. Stabbed once in his chest. Killed while walking from his parked car to the apartment block entrance. Neighbours heard him screaming 'Oh, God. Someone please help me!' It was newsworthy. Sal Mineo was a two-time Oscar nominee. Before *Exodus*, he'd had been in *Rebel without a Cause*. Amy Kaplan thought that in his role as moody Dov Landau he looked like he'd just walked off the set of that legendary movie. The contact details in Sal Mineo's address book included Bette Midler, Harold Pinter, Twiggy, John Schlesinger, Charlotte Rampling, Roald Dahl, Paul Newman. Etcetera, etcetera. The cops soon discovered Sal was gay. Lots of young males had dropped by to see Sal. On the night in question he'd dined at The Cock and Bull Restaurant [*sic*] with an old female friend plus his current male squeeze. Sal had gone on home alone, planning to meet up later. The lurid gay angle was a scarlet herring. The killer was a hard-up loser named Lionel Williams. It was a bungled robbery. Sal started shouting for help, so Williams stabbed him. Sal Mineo died of a massive haemorrhage. He was 37. He was interred in Gate of Heaven Cemetery in Westchester County, New York – Niche Bank area, 02 row, corridor 211, grave four.

33

In *Paul Newman: A Life*, Shawn Levy says that *for all the time the production spent abroad, the footage had a rushed feeling. Famously, Preminger left a shot in the finished film in which the shadow of the camera clearly passed over the trysting bodies of Newman and Saint.* Ellis hadn't noticed. He decided to watch out for it on his next viewing.

34

The movie's ending was invented. It is not in the book. Taha and Karen are buried together, while Paul Newman mouths platitudes about reconciliation. This final scene, writes Shawn Levy, was *meant to be an aria of mourning and hope. But despite Preminger's instructions, Newman played it more or less straight.* It was pointed out to Preminger that burying a man and a woman not his wife side by side flagrantly contradicted both Moslem and Jewish religious custom. The director didn't care. The message superseded realism. But that message was bogus. And afterwards the mourners go off to jump aboard trucks. They roar off into the future – to loot Palestine and drive its population from their homeland. The horror that lies beyond THE END is drowned in Preminger's syrup. *Zudoxe* is not a great film. Its hollow heart is rotten.

35

'The Zionist writer,' wrote Gassan Kanafani, 'must justify non-integration in the societies from which he came, and simultaneously justify the violent uprooting of Palestine's indigenous inhabitants. Such justifications in art are bound to expose the racist and fascist essence of the Zionist movement.'

36

Preminger's wife claimed that on the plane out of Israel Paul Newman turned to the director and said: *I could have directed this picture better than you.*

37

In 1980 Otto Preminger was crossing a street in New York when he was hit by a cab driven by a driver who was drunk. Preminger slid on to the hood. The driver kept going from 55th Street to the other side of Saks on 49th. There the driver braked and stopped. Preminger was thrown to the ground. His head smashed against the road surface. At first he seemed okay. Bruised and shaken he walked back to his destination, the restaurant La Caravelle on 55th Street. But it turned out he had suffered a serious trauma to the head, from which he would never recover. His wife said after the collision he *faded and faded and faded.* On April 23rd, 1986, he died of cancer of the colon.

38

Learning that Richard Dawkins had produced an analysis of Moses, Ellis borrowed a copy of *The God Delusion* from his local library. Dawkins describes the Bible (a 'weird volume') as *a chaotically cobbled-together anthology of disjointed documents, composed, revised, translated, distorted and 'improved' by hundreds of anonymous authors, editors and copyists, unknown to us and mostly unknown to each other, spanning nine centuries.* Ellis read Dawkins's account of how in the Book of Numbers God encouraged Moses to attack the Midianites. The Midianite cities were duly levelled and most of the population killed, apart from young girls, who were spared to become sex slaves. *Moses was not a great role model for modern moralists*, tartly remarks Dawkins. He notes that it appears the Midianites were the victims of genocide in their own country. But their name lives on in a popular Christian hymn, which exists to two different melodies, *both in grim minor keys*.

> Christian, does thou see them
> On the holy ground?
> How the troops of Midian
> Prowl and prowl around?
> Christian, up and smite them,
> Counting gain but loss;
> Smite them by the merit
> Of the holy cross.

Alas, poor slandered, slaughtered Midianites, to be remembered only as poetic symbols of universal evil in a Victorian hymn Richard Dawkins concludes. But this is all curiously like Zionism, the Palestinians, and Leon Uris's grotesque potboiler. Moses is a great Jewish hero, the man who led his people to the Promised Land. Zionism is every bit as fanatical and inhumane as the Old Testament. It blanked out the Palestinians, substituting Biblical fantasy and a virulently racist colonial agenda to seize an entire country by force of arms. Leon Uris's potboiler is no different to that Christian hymn. It's a celebration of destruction and dispossession, in which caring decent Jews want only to help the enfeebled Arab population who have neglected the land for thousands of years. But their decency is met only by monstrous savagery and fanaticism. Leon Uris turns history on its head. The Jews are saintly, the Palestinians are malodorous killers and torturers. A fertile and thriving land is portrayed as nothing but desert and swamp. The enormity of the Jewish theft of Palestinian has been successfully blanked out by the Jewish intelligentsia.

There is a vast moral blankness at the heart of modern Judaism, which can be found everywhere, from Paul Celan and Aharon Appelfeld to lightweights like Simon Schama. At the start of 1947 Jews owned just 7 per cent of land in Palestine. By 1950 they had seized 92 per cent of Palestine, including farmland, homes and businesses. It was colonial occupation on a scale and with a speed unprecedented in the history of colonialism.

39

Moses is a Jewish hero. Moses led the Jews out of Egypt. Moses was instructed by God. God wanted the Amorites, the Canaanites, the Hittites, the Perizzites, the Hivites and the Jebusites driven from their homelands. *The ethnic cleansing begun in the time of Moses is brought to bloody fruition in the book of Joshua,* remarks Richard Dawkins.

40

It's very noticeable that a reactionary like Richard Dawkins avoids acknowledging the importance of the Exodus story in Zionist ideology. He evades the alliance between Christian fundamentalism and Jewish myth in dispossessing the Palestinians of their homeland. Dawkins cites a study of responses to the story of the battle of Jericho recounted in the Book of Joshua. One thousand Israeli children were asked if they thought that Joshua and the Israelites had acted rightly or not in killing the entire population of the city – men, women and children – as well as their animals, and burning the city to the ground. Sixty-six per cent totally approved. Those who disapproved did not always do so for moral reasons. One child objected to Jews entering this Arab city 'since the Arabs are impure' and would contaminate the intruders. Another child objected to the killing of the animals, which the Jews could have taken possession of. A third child objected to the levelling of the city, which could simply have been repopulated with Jews. But having exposed the racism and moral void at the heart of Israeli culture and education (a rottenness exposed with much greater rigour and detail by Nurit Peled-Elhanan in her book *Palestine in Israeli School Books: Ideology and Propaganda in Education*) Richard Dawkins feels obliged to add some supposed balance. He adds: *It is, I suppose, not unlikely that Palestinian children, brought up in the same war-torn country, would offer equivalent opinions in the opposite direction. These considerations fill me with despair.* Two sentences which expose what a mealy-mouthed equivocal right-wing liberal Dawkins is, under his rationalist bluster. He daren't badmouth Israelis without rushing to slander Palestinians, for 'balance'. He offers no proof that Palestinian children are as prejudiced as their Jewish counterparts. And he reduces the conflict to one of theological prejudice rather than colonialism and sectarianism. By his timidity Dawkins is on the side of repression, not the side of liberation. No wonder that the paperback edition comes bearing the encomium *A magnificent book, lucid and wise, truly magisterial – Ian McEwan.* A novelist who was consumed with anguish after 9/11 and who had remarked that Russia's invasion of Ukraine made his blood boil but who so far had stayed silent over Israeli atrocities in Gaza, in which the British government was deeply complicit.

41

Ellis turned next to *Say What Happened: A Story of Documentaries* by Nick Fraser. He'd come across a reference on the internet which implied the book had something to say about Preminger's film. But it turned out that *Exodus* was a 2016 BBC TV documentary about refugees from Africa attempting to get to Europe. Ellis would have given up on the book but then he realised it had a section on Kevin Macdonald's film *One Day in September* (1999), about the abduction of eleven Israeli athletes at the 1972 Olympics by a Palestinian liberation group. According to the blurb, Nick Fraser was a man who 'created BBC Storyville, producing films that won Oscars, BAFTAs and Peabody Awards'. Fraser thought *One Day in September* was wonderful. He criticised Edward Said, who had summarised this documentary as 'bad politics, bad film-making'. *I felt at the time his observations were misplaced, and after watching the film again the day after the 13 November 2015 terrorist atrocities in Paris, I still do.* One Day in September *does give voice to the distress of the wife of the murdered Israeli fencing coach Andre Spitzer, and who would now suggest that was a bad idea?* Well, Ellis Sharp would, for a start. Ellis objected to yet another representation of Israelis as victims rather than violent sectarian thieves. Zionism was a violent racist ideology which had always planned to dispossess the Palestinians of their land and had accomplished it through extreme violence, including gang rape and repeated massacre. Those who resisted Zionism were not terrorists but colonised victims responding to Zionist violence, quite legitimately. It was characteristically meretricious of a BBC hack like Nick Fraser to juxtapose the events at Munich in 1972 with the utterly unrelated killings in Paris in 2015. That kind of collage technique was a familiar one when it came to smearing the Palestinians. Nick Fraser was a type. He thought of himself as liberal and fair but he functioned inside a comfortable space where certain frames were never transgressed. Why was there not a single documentary about any of the massacres committed by Jews against Palestinians in Israel? Why had there never been a single documentary about the history of political Zionism and its long project to steal an entire country? Nick Fraser was not the kind of person who would ever ask himself these questions. Ellis dug out his copy of Simon Reeve's book *One Day in September*. He looked up Ankie Spitzer. She was a Dutchwoman who'd married a Romanian Jew. Neither of them had been born in Palestine but both were happy to indulge their sectarian privileges as members of the ruling religion. *Ankie, a vivacious free spirit, returned with Andre to Israel and the couple moved to the north, on the border with Lebanon, where Spitzer founded the Israeli fencing academy in a group of derelict buildings.* Ah, yes – derelict buildings. No one ever asks who once lived in those derelict buildings, where European colonists turn up to occupy them. Or how they came to be empty.

42

The first scene of Preminger's *Zudoxe* melts from Eve Marie Saint's immaculate figure into the dockside at Famagusta. To the left of the frame is a British soldier, with a rifle slung over his shoulder. A line of Jews file past. One of the Jews is carrying a chess board. Behind him is BCK – blonde cutie Karen. Cut to Eve Marie Saint arriving in her taxi, which has to wait. What is going on, she asks the driver. *A prison ship has arrived full of Jews for the camps.* A continuity between the camps of the Nazis and the camps of the British is subliminally insinuated, and reinforced when we get to see the camp, with its barbed wire fence and watchtower. Impetuous and brave Dov Landau – the cuddly, comical, loveable face of the Irgun – attempts to escape but is quickly caught. Eve Marie Saint arrives at the house of her late husband's dear friend, the British commander, played by Ralph Richardson. We learn that her husband was a news photographer, heroically killed for the sake of an action shot. (He was photographing an attacking fighter plane – although quite which country this plane was from is something of a mystery, since Mandate Palestine was never attacked by a foreign power. Presumably an RAF pilot mistook him for a Palestinian.) We learn that Eve Marie Saint – from now on let's call her the Saint – was pregnant and the shock of her husband's death caused her to miscarry in Jerusalem. The Saint confides that Jews make her 'feel strange' but when Ralph Richardson's brash anti-Semitic assistant hints that Richardson may be Jewish she decides to help out at the internment camp, using her nursing skills. It is night. Paul Newman jumps from a boat and swims ashore. Next day the Saint arrives at the camp. We witness a comic scene between moody, angry, impetuous Dov Landau and sweet, calm, loveable BCK. Then Ellis put the movie on pause and went off to eat a packet of salt and vinegar crisps. His favourite flavour.

43

The Saint takes BCK to the beach. She's described as a 'child of light'. So blonde, so cute, so caring, so gosh-darned *nice*. She will be murdered by an Arab, to show the audience who is good and who is bad. Meanwhile brave, bold Ari is planning to get 611 Jews off Cyprus and on their way to Palestine. He demands the seemingly impossible of his awed associates. 'This isn't the Red Sea,' one of them says. One of them says 'He thinks he's Moses.' But he is. He's the leader of men, the one who gets things done. The bronzed handsome hero. The love interest for the Saint. Blonde American non-Jewish woman falls for our sexy Haganah hunk. The violent sectarian expulsion of the Palestinians from their land is dressed up as a Mills & Boon romance. Paul Newman plays it deadpan. He puts no emotion into the role. He didn't know or care about Palestine and its history. He just wanted more nuance. A one-dimensional hero is a hero constructed out of cardboard. Leon Uris's potboiler is for simpletons. Easy reading for the lazy. Everything is processed, explained, spelled out. Preminger's movie peddles some of the central Zionist myths. The Zionists have little money. They bravely stand alone, with the whole world against them. Garbage on a stupefying scale. A mountain of it. Tens of thousands of words, dead words, heaped high. Words to kill thought, understanding, historical truth and fact. Words processed by Dalton Trumbo into a serviceable script.

44

Ghassan Hanafani noted that Ben Ari in Uris's potboiler is basically the reincarnation of George Eliot's character Mordecai in *Daniel Deronda*. This was a novel which, in Kanafani's words, 'finally established the Jewish Zionist hero in English literature'. Mordecai envisions a future Jewish state as a wondrous utopia, bearing the culture and values of every great nation, 'a land set for a halting-place of enmities'. George Eliot – the classic liberal. In Kanafani's words, 'manoeuvring around the racist nature of the cause by trying to dress it up in a humanistic garb'. And as Kanafani also observed, within days of establishing the Jewish state in 1948 one of Tel Aviv's major roads was named after George Eliot, 'while the flames of the Palestinian catastrophe were still ablaze'. As for the culture and values of great nations: where

Europe, the United Kingdom and the United States were concerned, the final three months of 2023 and the first three months of 2024 showed that liberal culture was a thin, foul, putrefying skin wrapped around a comprehensive complicity in genocide.

45

The Bible. As Thomas Paine noted (*The Age of Reason*, 8th Pluviôse, 1794), there is the question of origins and voice and narrative perspective. *It begins abruptly. It is nobody that speaks. It is nobody that hears. It is addressed to nobody. It has neither first, second, nor third person.* As for what follows... *Whenever we read the obscene stories, the voluptuous debaucheries, the cruel and tortuous executions, the unrelenting vindictiveness, with which more than half the Bible is filled, it would be more consistent that that we called it the word of a demon, than the Word of God. It is a history of wickedness, that has served to corrupt and brutalize mankind; and for my own part, I sincerely detest it, as I detest everything that is cruel.* Apt, then, that this is the text which inspires Christians to support Zionism and Israel. Those sleepy English churches, including the one where that pudgy grasping celebrity landowner W. Shagspur is interred, which proudly advertise themselves as the local branch of Anglican Friends of Israel. Christians for torture. Onward Christian Soldiers, marching for racism, persecution and torture from sleepy tranquil Warwickshire.

46

When we read in the books ascribed to Moses, Joshua, etc., that they (the Israelites) came by stealth upon whole nations of people who, as the history itself shews, had given them no offence; *that they put all these nations to the sword; that they spared neither age nor infancy; that they utterly destroyed men, women and children; that left not a soul to breathe*; expressions that are repeated over and over again in those books, wrote Thomas Paine, and that too with exulting ferocity; are we sure these things are facts? Are we sure that the Creator of man commissioned these things to be done? Are we sure that the books that tell us so were written by his authority? Paine was incredulous at such a notion. The moral contradictions were blatant. God, in this account, was a petulant mass-murdering dictator. There were other objections. As Paine went on to note, the books attributed to Moses, Joshua, Samuel and others are books of *testimony*, and they testify of things naturally incredible; and therefore the whole of our belief, as to the authenticity of these books, rests, in the first place, upon the *certainty* that they were written by Moses, Joshua, and Samuel; secondly upon the credit we give to their testimony. But, Paine continued, the five books of Moses – Genesis, Exodus, Leviticus, Numbers and Deuteronomy – are spurious. Moses did not write them. They were not written in the time of Moses but hundreds of years later, by some very ignorant and stupid pretenders to authorship. The books are written in the third person. If Moses was the author and he wrote that *Moses was very MEEK, above all the men which were on the face of the earth* he was not meek at all but, Thomas Paine remarked, one of the most vain and arrogant coxcombs. In Deuteronomy there is an account of the death and funeral of Moses. We are told that Moses died at the age of 110 in the land of Moab and is buried in a valley there but the location of his sepulchre has been lost. To make Moses the speaker of this information would be an improvement on the play of a child that hides himself and cries *nobody can find me*. Nobody can find Moses.

47

And so Thomas Paine continued, tearing the Bible to shreds and exposing its inherent absurdities. What is the Book of Genesis? No more than *an anonymous book of stories, fables, and traditionary or invented absurdities, or of downright lies. The story of Eve and the serpent, and of Noah and his ark, drops to a level with the Arabian Tales, without the merit of being entertaining.* What's more the character of Moses, as stated in the

Bible, *is the most horrid that can be imagined. If those accounts be true, he was the wretch that first began and carried on wars on the score of or on the pretence of religion; and under that mask, or that infatuation, committed the most unexampled atrocities that are to be found in the history of any nation.* Moses, according to the Bible, gave an order to his captains *to commit war crimes against civilians: to butcher the boys, to massacre the mothers, and debauch the daughters.* What, then, is the Bible? *Nothing but a book of lies, wickedness, and blasphemy.* By 'Bible' Paine meant the Old Testament. *I have now gone through the Bible, as a man would go through a wood with an axe on his shoulder, and fell trees. Here they lie; and the priests, if they can, may replant them. They may, perhaps, stick them in the ground, but they will never make them grow.* And then Thomas Paine moved on with his axe to the trees of the New Testament.

48

Sudoxe, by Ellis Sharp, originally finished there, at section 48 (which was at that time section 47). He called his text *Sudoxe* to distinguish it from *Zudoxe* the novel and film. If they incorporated – as Roland Barthes might have said – the slashing violence of Zionism, Ellis's text expressed the hiss of disssssapproval. Ellisssssss's *Sssssssudoxe*. The hiss of a snake. Ellis liked snakes. He still remembered the travelling snake exhibition on the quayside at Paimpol, all those years ago.

49

Sudoxe had been drafted as a chapter in an unfinished novel, some years ago. Later, it was expanded, with a view to making it a stand-alone piece. But Ellis had abandoned it. *Night Architecture* had also originated as a much shorter piece, under 6,000 words. Ellis had subsequently tinkered with it, then set it aside, to be rewritten at some later date. He knew he needed to be in the right mood. Meantime other writing projects kept getting in the way.

Only in November 2023 did the moment seem right to rework both pieces. It also seemed like a good idea to set them side by side, in a single slim volume.

50

As history intervened, Ellis found out more about Leon Uris and the writing of his bestselling Zionist propaganda book. One detail shone out. On his research trip to Israel in 1956, fuelled by the enthusiastic co-operation of the Zionist state, Leon Uris was taken on a trip to visit a kibbutz named Nahal Oz. It was a sexy place to visit and popular with foreign journalists. Nahal Oz was founded by soldiers on farm land previously owned by Palestinians. The families who had once lived there were forced out and now lived nearby, in Shejaiya, Gaza. They were close enough to see their old fields, now stolen by Jews. Sometimes they crept back to harvest their crops. They were shot at and driven back into Gaza. Wikipedia will tell you that 'Arabs' crossed from Gaza to 'conduct petty theft' – which is a curious way of describing the dispossessed returning to their stolen property, now occupied by violent racist Jewish thieves. In reality Nahal Oz was the living embodiment of Jewish racism, militarism, violence and land theft. But the Israeli troops impressed American reporters. US television featured the kibbutz on a popular show, calling it a 'stockade'. It was practically a frontier town in a Western! The young Jewish soldiers – so handsome, so close to danger! In Gaza lived the equivalent of the Red Indians. The trip which the Israeli state laid on for Leon Uris to Nahal Oz was not innocent. Earlier in the month, after Egyptian troops on the Gaza border shot dead three Israeli occupation troops, the Israelis shelled the middle of Gaza City, slaughtering 58 civilians in the standard Zionist-Nazi revenge executions. On 29 April 1956 a settler 'security officer' on patrol was killed by Palestinian freedom fighters, who'd crossed from Gaza. Israelis swooned with their usual sense of outraged victimhood. Sexy eye-patch-wearing war criminal Moshe Dayan rocked up for the funeral. He was at this time chief of staff of the so-called Israel Defence Forces (an Orwellian euphemism reminiscent of the renaming of the British 'War Office' as 'The Ministry of Defence'). Dayan was there for PR purposes, to deliver a eulogy at the graveside. Leon Uris was there to hear him. It was lachrymose guff of the sort that sociopathic Zionists adore. 'Have we forgotten that this group of young people dwelling at Nahal Oz is bearing the heavy gates of Gaza on its shoulders?' spoketh ham actor Dayan. 'Beyond the furrow of the border, a sea of hatred and desire for revenge is swelling, awaiting the day when serenity will dull our path, for the day when we will heed the ambassadors of malevolent hypocrisy who call upon us to lay down our arms.' In other words, the dispossessed Palestinians posed a threat which called for massive military deterrence. The oppressive, violent Jewish state required armed readiness at all times. This fatuous and hypocritical eulogy was instantly reproduced as a state classic, equivalent to the Gettysburg Address. It made a huge impression on Uris and he reworked the Nahal Oz mythology at the end of his novel, where it becomes 'Nahal Bidbar' and Karen is cast as the tragic Jewish victim of barbaric Arab violence. Uris also drew on a feature about Nahal Oz in the popular general interest American magazine *Coronet*. This falsely portrayed the kibbutz as having been built on 'barren desert'. *Coronet* claimed that the brave occupants of Nahal Oz 'refuse to be bullied off their land' by 200,000 Arabs who linger on in 'filthy tent camps, unwanted by their host country'. (Astonishing chutzpah to define Israel as a 'host country' for Palestinians!) What's more, *Coronet* informed its readers, these lingering and nameless Arabs pass their days 'in resentful reverie'. Their idleness inspires only hatred and 'the energetic settlers of Nahal Oz are the closest objects of their hatred'.

51

The history continues: belligerent and violent Zionism versus Palestinian resistance. Writing this fifty-first part of *Sudoxe* in December 2023 it is too early to know exactly what occurred on the morning of Saturday 7 October 2023. The Zionist lie machine pumps out a perpetual mist. But it may be the case that up to fifty members of the Palestinian liberation forces broke through the separation fence around Gaza and stormed the military base near Nahal Oz. They fought their way inside, killing perhaps sixty-one Israeli troops. (These army representatives of a violent blood-drenched militarised settler state would later be sanctified by the elites of the Western world as 'innocent Israelis'.) Some members of the resistance reached the kibbutz and engaged in a shoot-out with Border Police and kibbutz security personnel. It is reported that twelve members of the Nahal Oz settlement were killed, along with Border Police and the security personnel. Members of the Palestinian resistance also died. The full facts will probably not be known for many years, although doubtless a sanitised Israeli version will be made available to right-wing Western authors. In a year or so, Ellis thought, commercial publishing will be awash with instant histories and memoirs promoting a Zionist perspective. Already the word 'massacre' is strictly reserved for Israelis killed by Palestinians. This convulsion of empathy for dead colonists among European, British and American politicians, along with the priests of capitalism (Vice-Chancellors and suchlike), was repellent after decades of indifference – or indeed direct complicity – in Palestinian suffering at the hands of the violent sectarian Jewish state. And while Nahal Oz is now once again sanctified by Israel and the West, its twin, Shejaiya, is forgotten, marginalised, shunned – even though on Saturday 2 December 2023 the Israeli Occupation Forces carried out a massacre there. An area of fifty houses and apartments was flattened, killing an unknown number of residents. Some social media sites give the figure of 300 dead. It might be accurate, it might be exaggerated. The facts are currently elusive. There is no heavy machinery to excavate the corpses. There is no one to report on the facts. Instead Israeli tanks cruise through the ruins. Jewish soldiers loot Palestinian properties, as befits a nation of thieves, whose nation is built on stolen land and stolen property. Who would have thought that 67 years after Leon Uris took his tour of Israel, the same two place names would surface, and the same enduring injustice would continue at the hands of the same violent, atrocity-sodden state?

52

Philip Roth's first marriage was to Maggie Martinson. Among other things he acquired a stepson, Ronald, who seemed to him barely literate. Roth persuaded him to read *The Red Badge of Courage*, which they then discussed. Roth found the boy 'emotionally goofy, far from quick-witted'. One day Ronald displayed a swastika. As a consequence Philip Roth made him read *Zudoxe*.

Roth's first book, *Goodbye, Columbus*, came out a year after Uris's book. A collection of five stories plus a novella. 'The real novelty of Roth's view of American Jewish life, circa 1959', writes Claudia Roth Pierpont in *Roth Unbound*, 'was its absence of any sense of tragedy or oppression.' Roth treated both working-class Jews and affluent country club Jews comically. He mocked them. Jews could be successful, exciting, silly. *Green lawns, white Jews*. This literary debut struck Ellis as sociologically interesting. The American Jewish community was divided about Roth. He later dryly remarked that in some Jewish circles *Goodbye, Columbus* was regarded as his *Mein Kampf*. He was accused of anti-Semitism and being a self-hating Jew. Remarkably, 59 years later, in her trashy book *Antisemitism* – Ellis was delighted that spell-check did not like that Zionist spelling of anti-Semitism – the ghastly Zionist harpy Deborah Lipstadt identified Roth as a 'latent' anti-Semite. According to Israel-worshipper Lipstadt, Philip Roth used shockingly negative stereotypes of Jews. An ignoramus like Lipstadt probably wasn't aware of Isaac Singer's retort to critics who complained about his Jewish characters who were thieves and whores: 'Shall I write about Spanish thieves and prostitutes? I wrote about the thieves and prostitutes that I knew.' *Goodbye, Columbus* won the Harry and Ethel Daroff Memorial Fiction Award for the best work of Jewish fiction in 1959 at the annual meeting of the Jewish Book Council of the National Jewish Welfare Board. The award for best work of poetry was won by Amy K. Blank for *The Spoken Choice*. Ellis wondered what had later happened to Amy K. Blank, not a poet he'd ever heard of. (The internet supplied the answer.) The previous year the award for the best work of Jewish fiction went to Leon Uris for you-know-what. David Boroff, who served on the jury for the 1959 award, wrote that American Jews were divided between the non-sophisticated and the sophisticated: 'You are given a choice: Leon Uris or Philip Roth.'

54

Leon Uris joined the marines as a teenager after the attack on Pearl Harbor. War provided 'an escape from a desultory adolescence shuffling between his divorced working-class parents' (Amy Kaplan, *Our American Israel*). He served as a field radio operator in the Pacific campaign. There he caught malaria and was sent back to the United States. On his research trip to Israel he enthused that the state was 'a nation of young marines'. The author jacket-photo used for the first edition of *Exodus* showed the author posing by a jeep, dressed in military fatigues and boots, with a machine gun clasped in his left hand. It was captioned 'with a patrol in the Negev desert'. Leon Uris worshipped guns, masculine strength and combat. He invents a hero who is admiringly described as a 'strapping six footer with black hair and ice blue eyes who could be mistaken for a movie leading man. He doesn't act like any Jew I've ever met.' Uris's Haganah hero Ari Ben Canaan is hard, powerful, brave, tough, fearless. He's as indestructible as a cartoon superhero. The opposite of soft. Leon Uris found Anne Frank's bestselling diary repellent. In 1958, after watching the Broadway adaptation of the diary, he wrote: 'I do not like to see Jews hiding in attics, and feel there is something far more decent about dying in dignity which is, of course, the choice that every Jew had.' Jews shouldn't hide. They should fight. In *Zudoxe* he cast Karen Hansen Clement as an alternative to Anne Frank. Karen falls in love with child veteran Dov Landeau. She dies defending a settler outpost. Dov becomes a terrorist. Uris disliked the Frank family's message of forgiveness. He hoped that 'this type of Jew has ceased to exist forever.' He promoted The New Jew: vigorous, manly, combative. Leon Uris also deplored the anti-war tendency in fiction. He loathed Norman Mailer's *The Naked and the Dead*, James Jones's *From Here to Eternity* and Herman Wouk's *The Caine Mutiny*. He called their work 'degradation and slime'. He was disgusted by what he called 'the "ain't war hell" school of writers'. War wasn't hell. It was paradise. Strong men bonded. Strong men found a testing ground for their masculinity. Leon Uris also detested the new Jewish writers. Saul Bellow. Bernard Malamud. Philip Roth. Writers 'who spend their time damning their fathers, hating their mothers, wringing their hands and wondering why they were born'. Man up, creeps! Leon Uris said their writing 'makes me sick to my stomach'.

55

Running for president in 2008, both Barack Obama and John McCain told Jewish voters they were fans of Leon Uris.

56

Tom Hanks once remarked that Uris's fiction taught him to feel history in a way no high school teacher ever did.

57

Zudoxe was reprinted 87 times and remains in print today. The cover of the Bantam Books paperback carries endorsements by *The New York Times*, which praised its account of 'the triumphant founding of the new Israel', and the *Chicago Tribune* ('A rich novel of Israel's birth').

58

In 2015 Vice President Joe Biden introduced Barack Obama at a celebration of Israel's independence day, telling the audience, 'As a young man, he grew up learning about Israel from the stories of Leon Uris in *Zudoxe*.'

59

Uris's book 'had nothing to do with reality,' said Yehiel Aronowicz, who was captain of *Exodus*, the ship. '*Exodus*, shmexodus.'

60

The only thing Yitzhak Laor the Israeli poet and author of *The Myths of Liberal Zionism* remembered about *Zudoxe* was the moment when Ari Ben Canaan lowered the shoulder strap of Kitty's nightgown and cupped her breast.

61

In the 1990s Shereen Sarick worked at a synagogue in Aspen, Colorado, where she tutored children for their b'nai mitzvahs. They included Rachael and Conor Uris. In thanks, their father, Leon, gave her a luxury leatherbound copy of *Zudoxe*. Shereen Sarick said the book made the story of Israel 'come alive'. The next year she jetted off to Israel on holiday. 'That was the beginning of my love affair with Israel,' she said. She returned over twenty times. So many times she couldn't remember exactly. Maybe thirty. A classic instance, thought Ellis, of a morally blank American Jew exercising her privileges to visit a land denied to the people it was stolen from. She reminded Ellis of the British novelist Clive Sinclair, another unbearably smug and complacent Jew who'd similarly embraced and celebrated a violent authoritarian state which gave him a good time as a member of the ethnic elite.

62

Shereen Sarick took her son to Israel for a few months when he was a young teenager. He didn't share her enthusiasm. It seems he was hostile. 'Now we can't talk about Israel,' she said.

63

Even as he was writing *Sudoxe*, Ellis discovered that the text was being enlarged by the latest Israeli atrocities in Gaza. He read that the 282nd Artillery Regiment's 411th Battalion crossed the border with its self-propelled M-109 howitzers, to aid the 188th Armored Brigade's offensive on Gaza City's Shejaiya neighborhood. The troops shelled more than 20 buildings in Shejaiya and also deployed flares and smoke shells to assist the ground forces.

64

Loen Uris was hostile to the views of his impoverished Russian-Jewish father, William Yerusalimsky. The surname was abbreviated to Uris by an Ellis Island official. The son 'created works full of aggression, profanity and the simplistic worldview of a cowboy movie'. No coincidence that in 1957 he wrote the screenplay for the Hollywood Western classic *Gunfight at the O.K. Corral*.

65

Mr Tough Guy lived in California, in a house by the ocean. Later Leon Uris moved to a ski chalet in Colorado. The man who promoted Israeli as the homeland of diaspora Jews preferred not to live there.

66

Ellis looked at yet another photograph of a dead Palestinian baby, the corpse scorched, covered in dust, falling apart. BBC News, true to its foul history, was careful to shield viewers from the reality of Zionist atrocity. For BBC News the Jewish settlers, beneficiaries of a violent apartheid state, were always promoted as the primary victims, and their quivering sensitivities got top billing. Genocidal violence directed against Palestinian children and women was of little interest to the BBC's reactionary expense-account news journalists on bloated salaries. Day after day after day revealed new massacres by the Zionist army – whole families crushed to death under rubble – but the BBC never used the word *massacre* or *Zionist* or *genocide*.

67

In March 1961 Philip Roth was invited to speak at Loyola University in Chicago. He began by mocking the idea of the Jew as a cultural hero, with reference to Pat Boone's theme song from the new movie *Zudoxe*. Listening to it on the radio Roth remarked that the DJ had described it as the only authorized version of the song. 'Authorized by what? For whom? Why?' Roth acidly recalled that the song *Zudoxe* had been preceded by the movie *Zudoxe* which had been preceded by the novel *Zudoxe*. 'However you slice it,' he commented, 'there does not seem to be any doubt that the image of the Jew as patriot, warrior, and battle-scarred belligerent is rather satisfying to a large segment of the American public'. Roth was in a combative mood. He quoted from Leon Uris's *New York Post* interview, saying that he'd been sent a copy by a woman who demanded an explanation for the 'anti-Semitism and self-hatred' which she'd discovered in *Goodbye, Columbus*. Ellis smiled another bleak smile, wondering if this angry moralist had been Deborah Lipstadt. He looked at Lipstadt's Wikipedia entry. She'd have been about fourteen at the time. Another of those authorial smiles. Maybe her furious defence of the Zionist entity had started early. Roth quoted Leon Uris's claim that during the course of his research for *Zudoxe* he experienced 'a revelation'. This sensational discovery was that 'we Jews are not what we have been portrayed to be. In truth, we have been fighters.' Roth described this statement as being 'So bald, stupid and uninformed' as to be 'not even worth disputing'. He cited the opinion of Yehiel Aranowicz, captain of the actual ship the *Exodus*. 'The types that are described in [Uris's novel] never existed in Israel,' the captain insisted. 'The novel is neither history nor literature.' But away from this local controversy the movie had an edge that Uris's humourless novel lacked. The screenplay supplied moments of comic irony. It included a reference to the Boston Tea Party, to bond Zionism with US history. And most of all, of course, it cast handsome all-American Paul Newman as the Jewish hero, Ari.

68

A year later Philip Roth participated in a panel of speakers at Yeshiva University in New York. He was the star. He was controversial. The mood of the audience was aggressive. The moderator's opening question was 'Mr Roth, would you write the same stories you've written if you were living in Nazi Germany?' The template for decades of defence of Israel. Jews must always be victims, who suffer. There is no such thing as Jewish bad behaviour. If you write about such matters – if you portray characters who are less than perfect – you are damaging the tribe. Jews have suffered so much, for so long. Never show them in a bad light. Furthermore a Jew who criticises Israel is a self-hating Jew. Only a Jew who identifies with Israel is a true Jew. Here, the Nazi genocide is the Ace in the worn, blood-stained Zionist pack of doctored cards. Remembrance is only permitted to take the form of an insistence that anti-Semitism is a mystical, inexplicable contagion that only the Jewish state can protect Jews from. To criticise Israel is by definition to engage in anti-Semitism. The only true history of Israel is the Leon Uris version.

69

Philip Roth told his audience at Yeshiva University the USA didn't remotely resemble Nazi Germany. He referred to Emmanuel Rackman, president of the Rabbinical Council of America, who had written to the Anti-Defamation League about Roth, asking 'What is being done to silence this man?' Rackman had added, with a murderous wink, 'Medieval Jews would have known what to do with him.' Roth told his audience that people like Rackman had learned nothing at all from the Nazi genocide 'other than how to remain a victim in a country where he does not have to live like one if he chooses. How pathetic. And what an insult to the dead.' It was not something his audience wanted to hear. Roth was astonished by 'the colossal brutality' of his adversaries. 'I realized that I was not just opposed but hated.' He felt 'finally overwhelmed...the strength just ran out of me and I felt as limp as a rag'. He contemplated getting up and leaving but decided that would hand victory to his opponents. When he left the stage he was surrounded by a furious crowd. Someone shook their fist in his face and screamed, 'You were brought up on anti-Semitic literature!' Roth asked the protester what he meant. 'English literature! English literature is anti-Semitic literature!'

70

Rabbi Theodore Lewis of the Progressive Synagogue in Brooklyn informed his congregation that in writing about 'exciting and lucrative themes – adultery, sexual licentiousness, marital infidelity, lechery, and human depravity in general', Philip Roth was not writing about Jews. 'Roth *never* writes about Jews.' Because Jews are good people. Roth realised that 'the issue of Jewish self-definition and Jewish allegiance' was a subject which could produce 'aggressive rage'. Jews – American Jews – the kind of Jews who found his writing offensive to Jewish identity – were 'fanatically insecure'.

71

Emmanuel Rackman returned to the attack. He said that the novelist had 'earned the gratitude of all who sustain their anti-Semitism on such conceptions of Jews as ultimately led to the murder of six million in our time'.

72

Each day, as he revised and expanded *Sudoxe*, Ellis learned of fresh atrocities carried out by the Jewish state. Every day more Palestinian families were massacred. The industrial scale of the barbarism was extraordinary, as was the almost complete silence of the European intelligentsia. And the past continued to come alive again. 15 December 2023: The Israeli Occupation Force stated that it had destroyed the headquarters of a 'battalion' in Shejaiya. *Shejaiya!* It claimed to have discovered and destroyed a tunnel opening. A resistance fighter had been killed. Later came the news that three of the Israeli settlers captured by the resistance had been killed by the occupation army. The circumstances were as yet unclear but the IOF stated: 'Israeli troops identified three Israeli hostages as a threat and opened fire at them, killing them.' It seemed plain that the soldiers had mistaken them for Palestinians and promptly executed them. And where did this happen? One news report casually mentioned a suburb of Gaza city: *Shejaiya.* A name which meant nothing to the sleek, history-ignorant journalists of the corporate media. And leaving aside the resonance of that place name it confirmed what was blindingly obvious. The Israeli troops combined gloating Jewish supremacism with Nazi tactics. They were out for revenge on the Untermenschen. The Israelis had been shooting dead Palestinian civilians for months, with the support of butcher Biden, blitzkrieg Blinken, blood-sodden Sunak, Starmer, and the European Union.

73

You can always tell a Jewish supremacist by her vocabulary. *Shoah* instead of *Holocaust*. *Antisemitism* instead of *anti-Semitism*. Ellis looked at the cover of Deborah Lipstadt's meretricious book *Antisemitism*. Published in 2019 it purported to be A TIMELY ANALYSIS OF THE NEW ANTISEMITISM. But that concept was a fraud, invented by Israeli propagandists. Defend the violent racist Jewish state by pretending that the real racists were those who opposed it and who wanted equal rights for the dispossessed and repressed Palestinians! The blurb referred to 'the antisemitism now raging in the British Labour Party'. Which told you all you needed to know about Lipstadt's greasy, fact-free politics. Below the blurb a photograph of a crowd of protesters. No location or date given. In the foreground part of a flag, which was probably the Palestinian flag, against, further back, the yellow and green flag of Hezbollah. The Palestinian flag adjacent to a large banner showing Benjamin Netanyahu, with a Hitler moustache superimposed, above the word FASCIST. This was presumably intended to supply a chilling example of Lipstadt's supposed 'new antisemitism'. On the front cover a recommendation by the playwright David Hare: 'So welcome, so necessary, so clear'. Ellis had never warmed to Hare's work, long before he'd learned to distrust Hare's oily, status-quo-supporting liberalism. Lipstadt's *clarity* included such assertions that the Boycott, Divestment and Sanctions campaign was 'definitely' anti-Semitic and that Philip Roth traded in anti-Semitic stereotypes in his fiction (Lipstadt also grimly convicted Herman Wouk of this offence). 'This is not harmless humour,' thundered Lipstadt. A writer like Roth belittled Jews and women. It was debilitating. 'This manifestation of latent antisemitism spreads hateful and hurtful tropes and ideas.' And next thing, before you know it, people are criticising Israel! Oh horror!

74

Ellis bought a second-hand copy of Philip Roth's *Reading Myself and Others*. First published in Great Britain in 2007, it said on the copyright page. *Great Britain*– not a term you heard that often nowadays. The imperial undertone. The immodesty. But then Ellis looked at the copyright page of his own books. Oh well...

75

Roth's volume was an assemblage of interviews, essays and articles. The blurb said they revealed 'a preoccupation with the relationship between the written and the unwritten world'. Ellis smiled a thin, dry smile. He wondered what the critic and blogger Steven Mitchelmore would think of that assertion. Roth had always seemed at home in the world. His prose gushed fluently. He had complete confidence in his chosen forms, his language.

Ellis had purchased the book to try and find out more about Roth and Leon Uris. It included two essays from Roth's early career which reproduced the relevant texts. The first, 'Some New Jewish Stereotypes', was the text of his opening speech delivered at Loyola University, as described in section 67 of the narrative you are reading. A footnote revealed something not given in the sources which Ellis had consulted whilst writing this section of *Sudoxe*. (He hoped *whilst* was grammatically correct – it sounded better than *while*. Ellis knew that his editor – who had a zealous commitment to good grammar – would tidy up any ragged, slovenly edges of his text. Sometimes Ellis wrote very fast, as if shouting out the words.) The footnote said that one of the sponsors of the literary symposium at Loyola was the Zionist outfit 'the anti-Defamation League of B'nai B'rith'. *That* explained a lot about Roth's audience. The published essay was interesting. Roth remarked, 'So persuasive and agreeable is the *Exodus* formulation to so many in America that I am inclined to wonder if the burden that it is working to remove from the nation's consciousness is nothing less than the memory of the holocaust.' He went on to observe, 'One week *Life* magazine presents on its cover a picture of Adolf Eichmann; weeks later, a picture of Sal Mineo as a Jewish freedom fighter. A crime to which there is no adequate human response, no grief, no compassion, no vengeance that is sufficient seems, in part then, to have been avenged.' This resonated over six decades later. Israel dressed itself up as the appropriate response to the Nazi genocide – the embodiment of the Zionist dream of a Jewish state where Jews would be safe. But the Zionists were Europeans, reacting to European prejudice. Settling, literally, on a Middle Eastern country, wrenching it using extreme violence from those who lived there. Israel would always be the most dangerous place in the world to live as a Jew, deservedly so, since it was a state built on atrocity, spectacular theft, and extreme discrimination. Browsing social media, Ellis came across a definition of Israel as *an increasingly fanatical and insignificant foreign state, governed by the far-right, carrying on the killing of innocents and the dispossession of refugees on a historic scale.* Exactly so.

77

Meanwhile, as *Sudoxe* continued to expand, Gaza and its population continued to burn and shrivel. The same process applied to all artistic endeavour of this time – every musical note, every written word, every brush stroke, every captured image was committed against a backdrop of massive slaughter and torment. Ellis wondered how this would register, culturally, when it did, if it did. Where the European and American liberal intelligentsia was concerned silence and exclusion seemed the most likely consequence. Doze on. Chatter brightly. Emote. Snooze on the chaise longue. Blank out the screams with pleasant music. Some nice cultural air-freshener will suppress the stench of rotting bodies. Turn away. Avert your gaze. Position your delicate spine so that it faces the casual detonation and levelling of entire neighbourhoods, while you look in the opposite direction. The Washington DC skyline. A quiet mews near Grays Inn Road. The Atlas mountains. The beach at Goldeneye. Use ear plugs (or consume BBC News) and block the noise of the industrial mass murder of women and children and the elderly. The calculated murder of civilians by Israeli snipers. *At times it was a pretty rough go*, wrote Leon Uris, describing his field research for *Zudoxe*, which included the trip to Nahal Oz.

78

All the barbarism muffled by BBC News. Day after day after day. The BBC, which both failed to report the daily atrocities and remained intoxicated by dead settlers, sobbing settlers, wide-eyed settlers. It was the old, old trick. Settlers were humanised and given names and stories. Palestinians were just an anonymous mass. It was the basic text of the Western media's treatment of Israeli violence (and before that, the violence of the British army under Montgomery and others). And another media trick was to assert that anti-Semitism was dramatically rising and Jews everywhere were fearful. But the statistics were always questionable, produced as they were by Zionist organisations with connections to Israel. Even the painted slogan 'FREE PALESTINE' was clocked up as a shocking instance of anti-Semitism. And of course the Jews who claimed they were fearful of an imaginary new genocide were the ones who had nothing to say about the *actual* genocidal violence of the Israeli state. The biggest fraud of all was the Holocaust memorial industry, which was entirely in the hands of Zionists and non-Jewish reactionaries. 'Never again' had been exposed as a vacuous slogan, devoid of substance. Holocaust Day was itself a farce and a fraud – wholly performative. Its only purpose was to exploit the past on behalf of Nazionism. Ellis also found it interesting, gazing at page 21 of *The Times*, 9 December 2023, that the headline read: 'People are blaming our 11-year-olds for what happens in the Middle East'. It was a full-page interview by Damian Whitworth with David Moody, the head teacher of The Jewish Free School in London. Needless to say there was no substance to the inflammatory headline. What people? Where? Not said. Not said because it was untrue. The feature was the usual Zionist garbage. There was sob stuff about 'a school community left shocked and grieving by the October 7 attacks by Hamas in Israel and then frightened and bewildered by antisemitism [the Zionist spelling] in London'. Why should a school in London be perturbed by a resistance attack on a violent settler state which had been committing atrocities against Palestinian civilians since its inception? The answer, implicitly, was that this was a school where to be Jewish was to identify with the settler state. Later in the feature it was casually revealed that speakers at the school in recent weeks have included 'Lord Mann, the government's antisemitism adviser' and – wait for it – 'Aviv Kohavi, a former chief of the general staff of the Israel Defence Forces'. Ellis had never heard of Kohavi. It turned out that he had a long Wikipedia entry. He was a top IOF man, implicated in numerous assassinations and killings. That The Jewish Free School invited men like Mann and Kohavi to speak to Jewish children spoke volumes about the brainwashing these children were subjected to, in order to shape their sense of self as intimately connected with Zionism. It was another reason for abolishing all faith schools, along with private schools. Later that month Ellis read on social media about a school in the occupied West Bank where the children were coming out of school after exams on Wednesday morning, 20 December 2023, and they were met with sound grenades thrown at them by Israeli soldiers. This was the kind of sadistic brutality which would never merit a full-page interview with the head teacher in *The Times*. And this was the casual, everyday barbarism of the violent settler state which the children of The Jewish Free School were being taught formed a key part of their Jewish identity.

79

Another day of Zionist barbarism in the Gaza strip. Reading a tribute to Refaat Alareer, the Palestinian poet and educator assassinated by the Israeli Occupation Force, Ellis discovered that 'he lived in the Shujaiya neighborhood, east of Gaza City'. That name again...

80

20 December 2023. Ellis learned from social media that the Israeli army had simultaneously blown up 56 buildings in the Shuja'iya neighbourhood. He watched the video, shot by a Jew. A huge wall of billowing smoke rose from the shattered structures. The voice of one of the Israelis can be heard saying 'Brigade 828 sends it greetings to Shuja'iya and from here victory begins.' It was done to please the settlers who lived close to the fence of the Gaza ghetto. 'We want those who stand in Nahal Oz and Kfar Gaza to see in front of them that Shuja'iya is flattened.' That name again: Nahal Oz. If Orwell's famous image of the boot stamping on a face forever resonated today it was because the face was Palestinian and the boot was Jewish. Yes, no one combined a Nazi mentality with moral smugness more than Israeli Jews and their numerous supporters around the globe. Elsewhere on social

media Ellis learned that German arms exports to Israel increased by 1000% in 2023, with orders being fast-tracked during the war on Gaza. This was the German state's third genocide and demonstrated yet again that no nation had learned less from the Nazi genocide than Germany since 1945. It was a land packed with pious memorials to historic suffering, the primary purpose of which it appeared was to provide an alibi for genocidal Zionism's violence and theft.

81

21 December 2023. On his laptop screen Ellis read about another concocted episode of supposed anti-Semitism, which had occurred at the International Documentary Film Festival Amsterdam earlier in the month. Film-maker Mohammed Almughanni gave a speech about his forthcoming documentary centred on a Palestinian boy growing up in a refugee camp in Beirut. In the course of it he asserted 'From the river to the sea, Palestine will be free.' Francine Zuckerman, a Canadian producer and director who has worked with the BBC, was at the event. She told *The Daily Telegraph*: 'It was so devastating and so uncomfortable to be in that room that as soon as it was over I just ran out as quickly as I could and was in tears on the street because it just felt so offensive.' Ellis looked Zuckerman up on the net and discovered she was the director of a recent documentary *After Munich*, which yet again – think Spielberg – milked the death of settler athletes on behalf of the Zionist project. Francine Zuckerman was yet another whiney, privileged Jew who was outraged by the notion that Palestinians might want justice and to return to the land stolen from them by European and North American colonists. Her moral blankness was evident in her emotional narcissism. She had no feelings to express about the barbaric industrial mass murder of women and children in Gaza. But she was not alone in this. The newspaper reported that 'International film-makers who declined to make their names public but whose identities have been confirmed by the *Telegraph* released a statement: "We, as Israeli and Jewish people feel

compelled to address the incident that transpired during the recent IDFA festival. During a pitching event, a Palestinian film-maker took the stage and expressed offensive sentiments, including the slogan 'From the river to the sea, Palestine will be free' and advocating for a return to pre-1948 borders."' Yes, nothing scandalised a Jewish supremacist more than the idea that Israel should grant equal rights to the people whose land and property it had stolen and that the apartheid state should be dismantled. This rabble of pampered, privileged Zionists were also outraged that a BBC hack had hugged Mohammed Almughanni. He had evidently been upset by the daily massacres in Gaza. Ellis looked up Mohammed Almughanni and discovered that he had been born in Gaza in 1994. So presumably he still had family and friends there. If so, some of them must surely have been murdered by the Israelis. Going further, Ellis was astonished to discover that in 2016 Mohammed Almughanni had directed a short documentary entitled *Shujayya*. That name again! Its content summarised as: *In Gaza, members of a typical family are thrown into disarray after a series of bombing attacks destroyed their home, killed some of the occupants and left others seriously injured.* The kind of violence blanked out by all those whining liberals of the West, for whom the horror only started on 7 October 2023...

82

Ellis began reading Philip Roth's essay 'Writing About Jews', first published in *Commentary*, December 1963. Exactly sixty years ago! A footnote by Roth explained that 'This essay evolved from remarks delivered in 1962 and 1963 at the University of Iowa Hillel House, the Hartford, Conn., Jewish Community Center, and YeshivaUniversity.'

83

Thursday, December 21, 2:20pm (GMT+3) *PALESTINIAN MEDIA: Clashes with heavy machine guns take place on the* outskirts of the Shejaiya neighborhood. *AL-JAZEERA: The Resistance launched a large batch of missiles toward the Greater Tel Aviv area, noting that more than 20 missiles were fired in two batches. AL-QASSAM BRIGADES: targeted an Israeli force holed up in a building in the Al-Mughraqa area in the central Gaza Strip with an anti-fortified TBG shell. HEZBOLLAH: We targeted the Doviv and Avivim colonies with "appropriate weapons" and achieved confirmed casualties. AL-QASSAM BRIGADES: We bombed crowds of enemy forces penetrating east of the city of Khan Yunis with heavy-caliber mortar shells.*

84

Thursday, December 21, 2:30pm (GMT+3) PALESTINE CHRONICLE CORRESPONDENT: *An air strike accompanied by artillery shelling targeted the Shejaiya neighborhood, east of Gaza City. Israeli air strikes are reported in the Ma'an area, east of Khan Yunis Governorate, south of the Gaza Strip. One Palestinian was killed as a result of the occupation's bombing and destruction of 'Hira Mosque' in Jabaliya Al-Balad, north of the Gaza Strip. Israeli aircraft targeted a house belonging to the Arouq family near the Sheikh Radwan Pool in Gaza City. Israeli aircraft targeted a house belonging to the Al-Arabid family in the Sheikh Radwan area of Gaza City.*

85

'Writing About Jews' was both interesting and disappointing. Ellis wanted to know Roth's further thoughts about Leon Uris and his bestseller but the topic was avoided. Instead Roth dealt with the argument that some of the stories in *Goodbye, Columbus* were damaging to Jewish people. His retort to his critics was admirable (it was obvious that a coarse, ignorant woman like Deborah Lipstadt hadn't read it when she revived the identical criticisms levelled against him decades before). What intrigued Ellis was that the controversy replicated what occurred nowadays when the wearisome charge of anti-Semitism was made by fanatically righteous Jewish sectarians against expressions of Palestinian solidarity. As Roth noted, his Jewish critics wallowed in the 'grandiose delusion' that Jewish life in the United States in the 1960s resembled Berlin in 1933, enjoying the 'paranoia' that it is *always* Berlin 1933 and consequently enjoying their self-appointed victim status. How like modern Zionists were Roth's critics back in the early 1960s who, he asserted, loved feeling 'helpless and threatened and in need of reassurance'. There was currently no shortage of affluent, privileged Jews in the West emoting about how upsetting it was to hear people chanting 'from the river to the sea Palestine will be free' whilst not being remotely perturbed by Jews slaughtering Palestinians on an industrial scale. And interesting though Roth's essay was, one thing was missing from Roth's reflections on his unhappy experience of addressing hostile Jewish audiences after *Goodbye, Columbus* came out. That was the word *Palestinians*. Even though Roth at moments adverted to the Jewish state he said nothing at all about the majority population whose country had been stolen from them by a minority of violent, murderously equipped sectarian Jews. At the end of the essay Ellis was astonished to read Roth's breezy reference to 'a symposium held in Israel held this last June at which I was present'. This was both playing to the gallery – guys, hey, I've *been* to Israel! – and a testament to Roth's own moral blankness. He exercised his sectarian privilege as a member of the master religion to jet over to the Jewish state, having nothing at all to say about the hundreds of thousands of Palestinians expelled from their home who were not permitted to return. They lived in refugee camps in conditions no Western liberal intellectual would have been able to bear for a day. It was an absence echoed by Roth's admirers. Ellis looked at the index of Blake Bailey's brick-sized biography. Nothing for 'Palestine' or 'Palestinians' but fifteen entries under 'Israel'. *Colonialism in contemporary indexes* – now *there* was a subject someone should write about! From Bailey's bloated tome Ellis learned about Roth's trip to Israel. The Zionist regime sponsored his four-day visit to attend a government organised literary symposium. Like Leon Uris, Roth was a privileged and pampered guest. 'I will go anywhere people are nice to me,' said Roth (yes, how easily you can purchase the services of an acclaimed corporate writer, thought Ellis – it was reminiscent of another profession). Bailey explained that the novelist 'planned to linger in Israel for a few weeks after the symposium (as the government had urged him to do), then spend the rest of the summer "someplace pleasant in Europe".' How perfectly splendid. Roth rocked up in the apartheid state, not apparently noticing that it was an apartheid state, for a public discussion of, among other selected topics, 'the alienation of the Jewish American intellectual'. (Alienated from what? Ellis wondered.) This was preceded by a meeting with that hideous, blood-soaked war criminal, David Ben-Gurion. The warcrim chuckled that alienation wasn't a problem in Israel. Roth and his fellow writers should immigrate. Why so? 'You see that street? It's a Jewish street,' said the warcrim. 'See that tree? It's a Jewish tree. See that bird? It's a Jewish bird.' By that logic even the rats were Jewish. But of course the streets and the trees were not Jewish. They were Palestinian. And Ben-Gurion was a violent, thieving European settler... What a fun time was had by all the members of the master religion! The Jewish writers discussed literature in Jerusalem, Tel Aviv and Haifa. But by now Ellis had had quite enough of the gripes of Roth.

86

Ellis glanced at a book he'd recently purchased second-hand, *Stateless in Gaza*, by Paul Cossali and Clive Robson. Published in 1986, it was an anthology of accounts by refugees in Gaza. Opening it at random Ellis came across a reference to the movie *21 Hours at Munich*, a 1976 American made-for-TV drama about the capture by a Palestinian guerrilla group of members of the Israeli Olympic team at the 1972 summer Olympics in Munich. It had been given a cinema release. The Gaza resident who'd watched it remarked, 'I can tell you that I came out of the cinema shaking with anger and frustration. The word Palestine or Palestinian was never mentioned and there was no hint at why, or what makes

Palestinians seize Israeli hostages. The commandos were portrayed as having no political motivation, mindless thugs, while the Israelis were heroes, standing up to international terrorism.'

87

Ellis reflected that nothing had changed in almost fifty years. Israelis still wallowed in victimhood, as did all those diaspora organisations devoted to connecting Jewish identity to the settler state, while those they murdered on a regular basis were represented as at best unimportant, at worst irrational. In reality October 7 was payback for over a century of dispossession, much of it accompanied by extreme violence. But Ellis knew there would be a flood of books, documentaries and eventually a Hollywood movie, which would be all about October 7. It would become a sacred anniversary, honoured by individuals and institutions which had been utterly indifferent to Zionist barbarism from its distant beginning. These manifestations would, very predictably, be about Israelis as the innocent victims of barbaric Arabs. The medium would be corporate publishing and the corporate press and television, each amplifying the other. And the Brutish Broadcanting Curpurration would be at the rotting heart of it.

88

Browsing the internet for *Zudoxe* references, Ellis came across a reference to Ethel Mannin. He read that 'Her 1963 novel *The Road to Beersheba* was expressly written as an "answer" to *Exodus*'. Elsewhere it was identified as the first Nakba novel. Cool. Ellis obtained a copy, second-hand. Mannin was a forgotten writer. Her fiction was long out of print. It looked like none of her fiction had ever gone into paperback. Although she'd been a feminist and a radical, no one had ever written a critical study of her work. She seemed to have led a long, interesting and at times adventurous life, but no one had written a biography.

89

Ethel Mannin seemed to have been big before the Second World War. By 1963 her fan base must have dwindled. *The Road to Beersheba* was about an episode fifteen years earlier in Palestine – a state erased from the map, the erasure having been marginalised both then and later by the British corporate media. The dustjacket blurb – probably written, according to publishing tradition, mainly by the author herself – explained what the book was about.

90

This is the story of the exodus from the small Palestinian town of Lydda, which was occupied by the Israeli troops in the Arab-Israeli war of 1948, when, with the refugees from Ramleh and the surrounding villages, some hundred thousand people, mainly women, children and old men – the young men having been rounded up – trekked through the burning wilderness to Ramallah, which was in Arab hands. Thousands died of sunstroke, exhaustion and thirst.

91

It was 1948 but it was also 2023/2024 – the same Jewish violence, the same Jewish atrocities. Except that this time it was happening in a connected, digital world and the victims were able to communicate some of what was happening to them.

92

This story of the other *exodus, the Palestinian exodus, has never been written before and the author's passion for justice and deep humanitarianism present it in its full pity and terror, in what we believe will be regarded as a memorable novel.*

93

An author's note added that *The Road to Beersheba* told *only a small part of the exodus of a million Palestinians during the Arab-Israeli war of 1948...The incidents described are as told to me by people who took part in this terrible trek. The characters are fictitious.* Ethel Mannin revealed that she had visited occupied Palestine and done field research for her novel. She had travelled *along the old Beersheba road as far as the Demarcation Line.*

94

But in 1963 the Nakba was little-known in Europe and the USA. The Leon Uris fantasy version of the founding of the Jewish apartheid state was what then dominated modern cultural memory, where that topic was remembered at all. The Nakba was not a topic to engage the reading public. Besides, the Zeitgeist had changed. It was the Swinging Sixties. Mannin had some serious commercial competition. Published that same year were *The Collector, The Girls of Slender Means, The Glass-Blowers, Horse Under Water, Inside Mr Enderby, On Her Majesty's Secret Service, Our Mother's House, The Spy Who Came in from the Cold, A Summer Bird-Cage, The Unicorn, The Bell Jar, Cat's Cradle, The Centaur, City of Night, Dead Fingers Talk, Dune, The Game-Players of Titan, The Graduate, The Group, The Man Who Fell to Earth, V* and *Visions of Gerard.*

95

Ellis looked at the list of proscribed 'terrorist' organisations on the British government website. **Harakat al-Muqawamah al-Islamiyyah** (Hamas) – This proscription was extended in November 2021. *Hamas is a militant Islamist movement that was established in 1987, following the first Palestinian intifada. Its ideology is related to that of the Muslim Brotherhood combined with Palestinian nationalism. The group operates in Israel and the Occupied Palestinian Territories.* It was, in short, a resistance group. The nauseating hypocrisy of the UK government was exposed by its account of Hamas's so-called 'terrorism'. *Hamas has used indiscriminate rocket or mortar attacks, and raids against Israeli targets.* The consequences were almost always trivial. Whereas the Israeli regime, armed by Britain, used extreme violence on a stupefying scale against Palestinian civilians, with a long record of mass murder. Hamas *frequently use incendiary balloons to launch attacks from Gaza into southern Israel. There was a spate of incendiary balloon attacks from Gaza during June and July 2021, causing fires in communities in southern Israel that resulted in serious damage to property.* These balloons were similarly inconsequential in their impact, and besides were launched against land which belonged to the Palestinians, not the settlers who occupied their stolen property. *Hamas recently launched summer camps in Gaza which focus on training groups, including minors, to fight.* Again, something the Zionist regime did on a much greater scale (as described, ironically enough, in *Zudoxe*). Ellis moved on to **Hizballah** (Party of God) – Proscribed March 2019. *Hizballah is committed to armed resistance to the state of Israel and aims to seize all Palestinian territories and Jerusalem from Israel.* In other words, to liberate the Palestinians. But those were just words, like a party political broadcast. It was important to distinguish between rhetoric and an agenda. The primary goal of Hizballah was to defend Lebanon from another invasion by the belligerent, expansionist Zionist state. As was partly acknowledged by the authors of the proscription statement. *Hizballah was established during the Lebanese civil war and in the aftermath of the Israeli invasion of Lebanon in 1982.* Exactly. It's an organisation set up to deter Israel. It's fundamentally *defensive.* Ellis managed a cold smile as he read the blood-spattered genocide-supporting UK government's splutter of indignation that *Hizballah continues to amass an arsenal of weapons in Lebanon, in direct contravention of UN Security Council Resolutions 1701 and 1559, putting the security of the region at risk.* That cold smile grew colder as Ellis read that *The US, Canada, the Netherlands, Israel, the Gulf Co-operation*

Council and Bahrain also designate the group in its entirety as a terrorist organisation. Gosh! A rabble of gangster states, torture states, the Zionist entity, the Great Satan, and the pusillanimous Dutch are opposed to Hizballah, and this underlines the case against this organisation! Laughable. Ellis went back to Tony Greenstein's website. Greenstein had been arrested by the British thought police for a tweet supporting Hamas's right to resist Israeli occupation. Greenstein commented: *The Terrorism Act 2000, if it had been in operation at the time, could just as easily have been used to proscribe the French and Czech resistance to the Nazis. It would certainly have been used to proscribe the African National Congress in South Africa which was classified by the United States as a terrorist organisation.*

96

The Road to Beersheba is divided into three parts titled *Exodus, Exile* and *Return*. The novel is centred on the story of Anton Mansour – a story of dispossession, exile and return. A contrast to the toxic fantasy of contemporary Judaism, whereby Jews around the world feel themselves entitled to a second country based on Biblical myth and the ideology of settler colonialism. Mannin's narrative begins when Anton Mansour is twelve years old.

97

On the first day of the new year, 2024, Ellis read a piece by Reuters, recycling an IOF hand-out. The genocidal Jews were now pivoting to the third stage of their ethnic cleansing. Israeli tanks and soldiers had now overrun much of the Gaza Strip. This will take six months at least, the IOF propagandist said. It will involve intense mopping-up missions against the terrorists. No one is talking about doves of peace being flown from Shajaia, the Jew sneered. Reuters explained that this was a Gaza district devastated by fighting. That name again: *Shujaiya.* As you would expect from Reuters: no history, no context.

The name kept getting repeated. It was at this time that one of the current survivors of the Gaza genocide wrote: *Nothing is sacred to Israel, not even the dead. Israeli forces destroyed Al Batsh Cemetery in Shejaiya neighbourhood in Gaza city. Mass graves filled with martyrs were dug up, and bodies were flung and trampled.*

99

Ellis obtained a copy of Ethel Mannin's 1964 travel book *Aspects of Egypt*. It described how she had a meeting with President Nasser. *I said I didn't consider the British Labour Party socialist.* That made Nasser laugh. He agreed that it was not. *And riddled with Zionism,* Ethel Mannin added.

100

They moved on to a discussion of occupied Palestine. *I said I had been in Gaza again, recently.* In her book Mannin only ever used the word *Israel* bracketed with apostrophes, to indicate its spurious and synthetic identity. It was a fake state. The pair discussed the military threat which Israel represented to the Middle East. *They have the means of waging bacterial warfare,* Nasser said. He said he believed Arab unity would only come about very slowly. *We went on to discuss the Israeli crime record and Zionist tactics.* Nasser told her that in 1956 the Israelis had sent one of his ministers a book. The parcel was opened by the man's wife. It contained a bomb and exploded in her face. She lived but was mutilated and blinded for life. On another occasion the Israelis had blown up an entire airliner, simply to kill one of the passengers. Nasser told Ethel Mannin that he himself had been the target of several Israeli assassination attempts. The couple talked for an hour and a half. She left with *the feeling of the man's innate sincerity and idealism.* She added: *I continued to think about this remarkable man far into the night.*

101

In *Aspects of Egypt* Ethel Mannin reminisced about her last visit to Gaza, which seems to have been in 1962. She wanted to see the old road to Beersheba because of an experience she'd had on a previous visit to Gaza. She had been visiting an orange grove when the body of a dead Palestinian shepherd had been brought back in a police van. The shepherd had been shot dead by an Israeli border guard – one of the innumerable casual racist murders committed by Israelis which have gone unrecorded in history. *The sunlight drained out of the brilliant day as we stood round in angry anguished silence looking – at the still face, at the blood on the white cotton* gallabieh . . . Ellis had no idea what a *gallabieh* was. He learned from the internet that it was an ankle-length robe with no collar, sometimes no buttons, and long wide sleeves. *We came to the Beersheba road, near the border... We turned into the road, off the main road, and drove up it until a U.N.E.F. soldier with a rifle with a fixed bayonet stepped forward from the checkpost shelter and stopped us. We called to him that we wanted to take a picture and he gave a sign of assent, but stood watching us, barring the way. We in turn watched an Israeli tractor working the land a few yards beyond the checkpost. I looked at the tense face of the man from Beersheba and looked away. Forty-seven miles along that forbidden road was his home, with foreigners living in his house. Fantastic . . . unparalleled in history. What was the use of saying it? Each knew what the other felt. The rage and bitterness. We turned away in silence and walked back to the car.*

102

Fantastic. Unparalleled in history. The rage and bitterness. The unending injustice.

103

Saturday 13 January 2024: *Three armed Palestinians trying to break into settlement killed*, says Israeli military. Israeli forces killed three armed Palestinians who were trying to break into a settlement in the occupied West Bank overnight between Friday and Saturday, the Israeli military said. The three Palestinians were armed with knives, a rifle and axes, reports Reuters, citing information from the official Palestinian news agency, Wafa. Two were 16 years old and the third was 19. The Israeli military said a soldier was wounded in an exchange of fire with the assailants as they breached the outer fence of the settlement Adora, near the settler-occupied Palestinian city of Hebron.

104

At 6.59am on Thursday 29 February 2024 Ellis woke to the beeping of his bedside alarm clock (an ancient, sturdy instrument with a broken second hand). He turned on the radio. BBC News continued its work on behalf of Zionist genocide. It gave top billing to a grotesque speech by the fanatical tax-dodging spiv Rishi Sunak, regarding alleged 'mob violence' by protesters. This, it instantly transpired, was rhetoric aimed at shutting down peaceful protests about Israel's genocidal violence against the Palestinian population in Gaza. For comment the Today programme platformed Dave Rich of the Community Service Trust (CST). The Today programme did not say that Dave Rich was an ardent and ubiquitous promoter of the Zionist state. It did not say that the CST was a Zionist organisation, which regularly produced lurid, highly questionable statistics about alleged surging anti-Semitism in Britain. Dave Rich's interviewer was fawning, giggling Nick Robinson, the epitome of a right-wing mediocrity in the costume of a court toady. One of the many Osrics of the corporate media. The risible 'interview' promoted two lies. Firstly that Britain was a seething mass of Jew hatred. The second was that 'the Jewish community' lived in a state of terror and intimidation. The Jewish community was code for the whining rabble of Israel worshippers and Jewish supremacists who ran every prominent Jewish organisation in Britain – including all those bogus Holocaust memorial outfits run by genocide-deniers and exclusively devoted to abducting the six million dead on behalf of Israel. This propaganda blocked out the news that the BBC chose to shun. Overnight more Palestinians had been slaughtered by the Zionist killing machine. Moreover there were *Reports that at least six more children have died of dehydration and malnutrition in northern Gaza,* from the UN Agency for Palestine Refugees (UNRWA). UNRWA said: *Unimpeded access across the Gaza Strip is needed now. An immediate ceasefire continues to be a matter of life and death.* News of no interest to a smug, plump, pampered stenographer like Nick Robinson. Something else: the latest fatality statistics from Gaza revealed that more than 30,000 Palestinians had been killed in revenge by the fascistic Jewish state. That figure did not include the uncounted dead rotting under the rubble or all those slaughtered on a daily basis in the occupied West Bank. Even as he wrote this paragraph Ellis learned of the latest Israeli atrocity: Palestinians queuing for aid in Gaza City had been massacred: *Fares Afana, the head of the ambulance service at Kamal Adwan hospital, said medics arriving at the scene found 'dozens or hundreds' lying on the ground. He said there were not enough ambulances to collect all the dead and wounded and that some were being brought to hospitals on donkey carts.* Unending barbarism, sponsored by butcher Biden and blood-drenched Blinken, blood-sodden Sunak and *Zionist without qualification* Starmer, and the leaders of the EU and the white European settler states of New Zealand, Australia and Canada.

105

The story of Anton Mansour. Lydda. Ellis planned to expand his analysis of Ethel Mannin's narrative, annotated with facts from Michael Palumbo's *The Palestinian Catastrophe* and Ilan Pappe's *The Ethnic Cleansing of Palestine*, supplemented with material from Tom Segev's Ben-Gurion biography. But he lacked the energy and the time. It was the last day of March, 2024. The text had run its course. Ellis had no stomach to go on, not now, not when Palestinians were still being massacred and now starved on a daily basis. Ellis decided he was finished with *Sudoxe*. It was time to set the text free. Let it snake its inconspicuous way along the blood-drenched gutters of rogue state Britain's contemporary literary culture. Last page. Finished unfinished. Full stop, final.

AN (UN)**END**(ING)